SNO-ISLE REGIONAL LIBRARY

APR   1998

W9-BXY-996

WITHDRAWN

WITHDRAWN

they're cows,
we're pigs

they're cows, we're pigs

by Carmen Boullosa

Translated from the Spanish by
Leland H. Chambers

Grove Press
New York

Copyright © 1991 by Carmen Boullosa
Translation copyright © 1997 by Leland H. Chambers

All rights reserved. No part of this book may be reproduced in any form or by any
electronic or mechanical means, including information storage and retrieval systems,
without permission in writing from the publisher, except by a reviewer, who may quote
brief passages in a review.

Published by arrangement with Julie Popkin, co-agent with Dr. Ray-Güde Mertin,
Literarische Agenteur, Friedrichstrasse 1, D-61848 Bad Homburg, Germany
Originally published in 1991 as *Son Vacas, Somos Puercos: Filibusteros del Mar Caribe* by Ediciones
Era, Mexico City

Published simultaneously in Canada
Printed in the United States of America

FIRST EDITION

Library of Congress Cataloging-in Publication Data
Boullosa, Carmen.
    [Son vacas, somos puercos. English]
    They're cows, we're pigs / by Carmen Boullosa : translated from
the Spanish by Leland H. Chambers.—1st ed.
        p.   cm.
    ISBN 0-8021-1610-8
    I. Chambers, Leland H., 1928–   .   II. Title.
PQ7298.12.O76S613   1997   96-40086
863—dc21

DESIGN BY LAURA HAMMOND HOUGH

Grove Press
841 Broadway
New York, NY 10003

10 9 8 7 6 5 4 3 2 1

To Alejandro Rossi
and to David and Gillian Berry Arango,
the newest of tiny newborns.

author's note

In 1678 *De Americaenesche Zeerover* (*The Buccaneers of America*) was published in Flanders. The story, now one of the most enduring in the literature of the Americas, traveled through time, place, many cultures and translations, each time bearing the stamp of its surroundings. For example, I noticed that in order to favor certain biases the Spanish translation of *The Buccaneers of America* was altered by expanding or abbreviating passages and reshaping the roles of some of the characters. And just when I thought that this version was essentially an authentic retelling of actual events, a more recent Cuban edition came into my hands, and its structure and wording had almost nothing in common with any version I'd seen up to then. All seemed to bear the signature of Alexander Olivier Exquemeling, native of Flanders, but as far as the identity of Exquemeling, a.k.a. Smeeks, goes, this remains rather in question, and there are those who maintain that the publisher or translator is the true author of the book.

What better point of departure, I thought, for a novel? The series of fictions before me allowed me to give free rein to my own very personal point of view. I first thought of making the book itself the principal character, but I ended by giving in, completely captivated, at the feet of Smeeks, by surrendering to Exquemeling, "the pirates' physician." The difficult, unstable terrain where the tale originated interwove with the mystery that carries a novelist into a novel, and so I entered the community of the Brethren of the Coast, into that first attempt to forge a socialist, antimonarchical society in the Caribbean. Their hatred for the Spaniards, their alienation from the European order, were very appealing to me.

But none of these reasons are sufficient to explain how this book came to make me its own, a vehicle for Smeeks, and forced me to retell it anew, to set it down on paper. We are all many things, hybrids formed of different identities. If truth be known, I am much more cow than pig. My natural affinity is with those of a more settled life, and I believe that not to defend the weak is the quickest path to ignominy. But even more important, I've cast my lot with the universe of the feminine. The Brethren of the Coast proclaimed the equality of all races, all nations, and were rather tolerant concerning all the sexes—except the female: women were forbidden in their community. In its series of adventures, this novel is then a laboratory of things feminine *in absentia* as much as it is a reminiscence of men who rebelled against a cruel order, an outlaw order, and ended by being as cruel and outside the law as the order they detested.

This is not, however, simply another translation of Smeeks's book. I have not falsified anything, but merely allowed the novel to conquer me, to secure for me the resources for entering into the complex world of the Caribbean, completely reenvisioning my own generational biases. For years my generation was fascinated by the Cuban experiment and by sexual freedom, and I would like to believe that it continues to be concerned with the liberation of women and the richness of androgyny.

In the explosive end of our own century, all human dreams seem mired down. But, like many others, I still have hope. Stendhal wrote, "After geometry, there is no better way to think than on the basis of events." Maybe that is why I wrote this adventure story, told from inside the rhythm of Smeeks's body: to delve into the silences in our history as well as into the validity of a dream that was unable to realize itself cleverly enough to escape the character of its time. Through Smeeks, I wanted to look into dreams destroyed in their time, to think actively, by telling a tale, perhaps, like Scheherazade, to stave off the arrival of death.

No one in this world who does not steal can live in it. Why do you think the judges and officers of the law hate us so? Sometimes they banish us, sometimes they have us whipped, and sometimes hanged, even though our saint's day may yet not have arrived. . . . It is because they do not want any other thieves besides themselves and their underlings around them. What keeps us free more than anything else is an ample stock of clever guile.

—Quevedo, *La vida del Buscón*

the slave

To be the slave who lost his body
so words might come to live in him.
To bear as bones innocent flutes
that someone plays from far away,
or maybe no one. (The breath alone
is real, plus the yearning to
decipher it.)
To be the slave when all are sleeping
and incite the persevering
splendor of the sibling lamp.
Always fearfully on watch
before the stars, unable to
equivocate when they awaken
though the world is under water
and night puts shadows on the page.

To be the slave, pariah, alchemist
of accursed metals—
transmuting boredom into agate,
into gold our human clay,
so no one will toss him to the dogs
when he yields up his share.
—Eugenio Montejo,
Alphabet of the World

part the first

which treats of the arrival of Smeeks
in Tortuga and how and with whom
he learned the trade of
physician and surgeon

one

See it? All of it have I seen. For good reason am I in possession of the eyes of J. Smeeks, to whom some attribute the name of Oexmelin and who, in public, not to bring attention to his person, calls himself Exquemeling, Alexander Oliver Exquemeling, even though my name is Jean Smeeks, or "Le Trépaneur" the times I was companion to J. David Nau on his expeditions, the same who was known as L'Olonnais among his own men and Lolonés to the Spanish, the son of a small merchant of Sables d'Olonne—hence his surname. I wandered about even when a child, with such long legs and a body so nimble and fleet that sometimes I would not be seen at home for several days at a time.

Hear it? I have heard all of it, because I also have Smeeks's ears. Together, eyes with ears, they will begin with me to relate the stories of Smeeks in the Caribbean and also of those I shared adventures with, such as the above-mentioned Nau, L'Olonnais, of whom I heard it said that he allowed himself to become an indentured servant to a colonist from

Martinique who was passing through Flanders and got him to sign a three-year contract for the West Indies, a brutal master, only good for beating him tirelessly, so that in a short while, although on Martinique by then, the youthful Nau soon found slavery unbearable. Yet it was a good thing he was there, else no other recourse would have remained during the voyage but to throw himself into the ocean headfirst. I can neither imagine what Nau did to get away from his master on Martinique, where it was quite as impossible for him to do so as on the broad sea, nor can I explain here how it was that he escaped from the island, since no one ever told me what stratagem he used (he that was so good at contriving them) for managing to take flight with some buccaneers from Saint-Domingue who were selling cattle hides on Martinique. He was attracted by the free life these men lead, loose in the forest, from what he had heard, without wives or children, for a year or sometimes two with perhaps a buccaneer or two for company. They care for one another if they get sick and they all share everything alike— sorrows, joys, whatever befalls them: a life spent in hunting and butchering the animals, drying their flesh in the sun and smoking it with green wood to sell to colonists on the neighboring islands or to Dutch ships and freebooters looking for ships' stores. They dress in a garment, loose-fitting, down to the knees, wherein the kind of material it is made of is difficult to make out, being covered all over with clots of dried blood; it is secured by a belt which often holds four knives and a bayonet. But when Nau finds himself amongst the buccaneers, the leader prevents him from going on his own and for several months keeps him, under the threat of death, as his servant, treating him so badly that he becomes ill; for those buccaneers are extremely cruel to their servants, to such a degree that the latter would rather be rowing in the galleys or sawing Brazilian lumber in Holland's Rasp-Huys than working for such barbarians. One day he is unable to follow his master because he is so sick, bent to the ground, nearly, under heavy bags of gunpowder and salt; a master so cruel that in a wrath he strikes Nau on the head with his musket, half killing him, and, thinking him really dead, he leaves him behind with the fireflies and three dogs for his only company. The fireflies illuminate the area around him on the dark nights, their bodies glowing with an intense light such as we have never seen emitted from any insect's body in all of Europe; and the dogs take care of him, feeding him by hunting wild pigs until, helped on by eating raw meat, he finds his precarious health is restored and wounds are healed, the animals with their kindness having rubbed away the effects of his master's beatings and soothed the fevers that he also owed to the vicious buccaneer's brutal treatment. For months Nau carries on a solitary existence, which is broken off when another pair of buccaneers run into him and they feel sorry for him and appoint him a buccaneer as well, teaching him first of all to eat cooked meat and prepare it as they are used to, the way the Arawak Indians do it, in the form called *boucan,* which we just described; and also to manufacture their own footwear, themselves fashioning their moccasins in the following manner: just after killing a pig or a bull, having flayed it they place their foot inside the part of the skin that used to go around the animal's

leg, fitting their big toe into the area where the animal's knee
used to be, bringing it up above the ankle about four or five
centimeters, and there it is tied; this done, they allow it to dry
on the foot and take on its shape.

Nau was a very capable hunter, but another form of life
called out to him, as it was more audacious, adventuresome,
and cruel, and thus he abandoned the company of the buccaneers, yet not without first splashing his erstwhile master's
brains on the ground of his hut, employing a well-delivered and
well-deserved blow of his ax as the man slept.

I was also an associate of Henry Morgan, the most famous of the English pirates in the Caribbean, who, according
to what I learned from the horse's mouth, was the son of a rich,
honest farmer but was disinclined to follow in his father's foot-
steps and so signed on with some ships bound for the island of
Barbados, with the intention of going into service with someone who later sold him. That is what I was told, but many years
after giving this out for a fact, Henry Morgan forced us—the
editor and myself—to add a paragraph in the book: "Exquemeling is mistaken concerning the origins of Sir Henry Morgan," it was necessary to incorporate into the English edition.
"The latter is the son of a gentleman of ancient nobility from
the County of Monmouth, and he has never been servant to
anyone except His Majesty the King of England." Well, do tell!
By that time the traitor Morgan was so rich and powerful that
he was able to appoint himself the son of whomever he wanted.
It is quite another thing for anyone to believe him. I, with the
eyes and ears of J. Smeeks, the only thing I can do in this

respect is not to speak at all about the traitor Morgan in this
book, and dedicate all its pages regarding our sojourn in the
Caribbean to the memory of le Nègre Miel and to telling about
Pineau, the men from whom I learned the profession and the
true Law of the Coast.

      For a pair of eyes and a pair of ears to fix images and
sounds in the temporal order in which they happen is no easy
task; their memory enjoys making fun of the tyranny of time.
But even though images may leap up pell-mell before us, like
the sight of birds pecking at the crabs and devouring them on
the sand of some Caribbean island (thus corrupting the flavor
of their tender flesh with the crabs' own bile that blurs the vision and darkens the minds of folk who eat them to excess), or
the sound of their strong beaks, like thunder crackling, breaking up their shells, I will attempt to rein them in and start at
the beginning of the story I wish to tell, with the moment
Smeeks sets his two feet on the deck of one of the thirty ships
of the French West Indies Company in a rendezvous at Cape
Barfleur, bound for Senegal, Terranova, Nantes, La Rochelle,
Saint-Martin, and the Caribbean; on a ship named the *Saint Jean,*
with twenty-five guns, twenty sailors, and 220 passengers,
headed for the island of Tortuga, whose governor in that year
of 1666 must have been Bertrand d'Ogeron, who would give
us more than one reason to hate him.

      We weigh anchor the second of May. Many other young
men like Smeeks are aboard, young fellows who have begged
on the streets, worked as servants, been sold away by their families; youths whom the colonist farmers or the Company have

engaged as indentured servants for a three-year stint: lured by the riches of the West Indies, the adventure, a new land both unknown and different, but above all, by the notion of getting away from Europe, so little generous to us. But the *Saint Jean* does not carry only sailors and youths; there are soldiers, too, signed on to defend the interests of the Company, merchants, older men who do not know exactly what they will face there, some with experience on many voyages but most of them undertaking their very first one, adventurers of various sorts, colonist farmers who have gone to bring back laborers, representatives of the King with their servants and secretaries who are making the trip in separate cabins . . . To be frank, Smeeks has enough to do with his own concerns without taking a close look at the *Saint Jean*'s 220 passengers: Smeeks does not spend time watching those who are going with him or those traveling in a different state; Smeeks uses this first stage of the trip, a time so different from that on dry land, more stretched out and monotonous, to try to catch up with himself. A few afternoons ago he was a boy of thirteen, wandering pointlessly around Flanders, sometimes as a servant if fortune smiled on him (even with unusually good luck, such as when I learned to read and write with a priest who seemed to think of me as more than a servant, and more than a boy), sometimes surviving by the skin of my teeth, carrying packages, transporting goods around the port—but always outside the house where I had grown up as a boy and which was neither my father's house nor yet my mother's, where I had never been treated decently or fed well enough to allow my stomach any peace, a house where I was no longer permitted to sleep, but around which I had taken to wandering. I knew it was senseless, served no purpose, as no one was waiting for me within, there was nothing for me there; nor were they disposed to continue putting up with a nuisance who was already thirteen years of age and who for the past five years now had already been scraping along on his own, tooth and nail, and who ought to continue scraping along on his own—and if he scraped up enough why should he not be bringing food home? My first job was as a servant, a servant's servant, to be more precise, but it did not last long because I had the good fortune to run into the priest who . . . But why keep going back? There in the patio behind the years is no recollection worthy of being brought into the present, nor anything that in any way helps along the story I wish to tell: the story of Smeeks in the Caribbean. So, to make headway, I will rejoin the voyage during which Exquemeling is trying to be reunited with himself, trying to get accustomed to the idea that he is the boy gazing patiently down at the grain of the wooden planks of the deck covering the hold where the youths sleep while aboard, as if in its striations he were gazing at the sea scraping at the stubborn pitch sheathing the hull below the waterline; though in reality, with his fixed stare, he is not gazing at this at all, as wood is not like the waters of the ocean.

One of those first afternoons, still somewhat disconcerted to realize I was on a voyage I had never imagined, never sought out, a voyage fallen out of nowhere on no particular day when I was drifting about without a glimmer of change in the seat of my poverty, as if the voyage were the fruit of the im-

measurably deep dreams of a magician who knew how to obtain substance out of nothingness, a voyage which materialized
only because I had heard about a man who was looking for hands
to indenture themselves with the French West Indies Company
and I'd gone to meet him—one of those first days aboard ship,
as we were saying, with my vacant eyes fixed on the striations
in the wood, one of the other youths with whom I share this
voyage approached. He seemed like a quiet, shy youth, moving
around very little, and then with hesitant, small steps, although
with body erect, avoiding all the talking and joking around; who,
when we went up on deck to pick up an earthenware or perhaps wooden bowl or saucer with our daily portion of hot food
(which was always most foully prepared by the older sailors and
cooked or boiled over an iron grate above hot coals on a bed of
sand on the deck, in huge cauldrons into which they reluctantly
tossed—apparently no one paid any attention to what was going
in next to what—garbanzos, rice, chunks of meat, garlic, ca-
pers, anchovies, almonds, prunes, chopped quinces, mustard,
dried fish, stale bacon, sardines, lentils, and not very much of
any of this, quite true, but all piled in together; in fact the only
things on the ship that were safe from the cauldrons were the
biscuits, honey, wine, and a cow we carried on board to pro-
vide milk and cheese for the privileged passengers—among
whom I was not to be found, of course. Together with water
for drinking, such were the provisions the *Saint Jean* carried for
those who belonged to the Company; but each passenger who
did not was responsible for his own supplies, and this often
without much sense of how it should be done, because their

improperly salted meat soon spoiled, their grain and biscuits rotted, and sometimes even the skins for holding their wine or water turned sour, reason enough that, throughout the crossing, these ears heard complaints time and again about the scant pleasures of their meals, heard painful laments from those who suffered hunger and wild thirst because of their lack of experience in preparing their stores while still on land), when, as I was saying, we were on deck to get our daily ration of hot food (mornings and evenings they sent biscuits and seeds down into the hold where we slept so we would be out of the way), he would stand off to the side as if he were a person of quality, the kind who normally eats with a silver spoon, although this was not so, as his impoverished manner of dress made clear, and would stand apart from the clusters of boors and cutups who used their fingers to shove this vile, nearly inedible food into our own rankled but always famished mouths.

It was not his odd melancholy bearing alone that made this youth so noticeable. He also stood out because of his beautiful features, though, if truth be known, it may be that I had not realized this before the event I am going to tell of. Like many of us, he had not the slightest notion of any hair on his face yet, but the rosy tone of his skin, which one would have guessed to be extremely soft, was much better than that of any of us. That afternoon I certainly was not thinking of this, of course, nor was I thinking of anything else: as if—in order to get used to the idea that I was the one who was embarked on the *Saint Jean* and headed for the island of Tortuga, which I had heard a little about but always in some garbled fashion—I needed to slip into a sort of mental vacuum, close to boredom. And that was easy enough to manage because by this time we had left dry land behind several days back, and the greater part of the time we spent shut up in what the crew pompously called the "company cabin" but which was nothing more than the ship's hold and from which they allowed us to emerge only to snatch a peek at the ocean during the space of time they were spoiling our appetites with their filthy stew. If not how oddly this particular youth struck me, yet must I have been plunged into thought about something, anything whatever, for the blow to have fallen so cunningly and efficiently on so unsuspecting a being: on me, poor Smeeks, who was rocked from stem to stern when what I am about to relate took place. For example, I should have thought how strange it was that he had drawn so near me, he who had seemed to reject close proximity to anyone whatsoever, at least insofar as our crowded conditions permitted; I ought to have reacted long before this event took place that later on caused me so much grief and so little profit. Yes, the youth's closeness should have disturbed me, but I did not see him; moreover, I certainly ought to have begun to wonder when he started to address me, and even more so at the tone of his voice. I do not know what he told me at first, but when he did succeed in getting my attention, he asked my name (I did not ask for his) and went on talking to me in his soft, gentle voice about things I did not believe important but that were pleasant and soothing while surrounding me with a friendly warmth which without equivocation I could call "trustingness," and which prevented his nearness, gradually growing, from having any negative significance for me, to the point where his body and mine seemed glued to each other at the ribs, and his unceasing, evenly placed words finally managed to impress themselves upon me only by the movement with which he expelled them from his mouth.

Suddenly, without the slightest violence but simply utilizing the rhythm of his speech, he grasped my hand and pushed it inside the clothing covering his breast, down to the skin, and at the same time, almost interrupting the sensation in the palm of my hand beflustered by the shape it was touching, he asked, looking me straight in the eye, "Have you ever touched a woman before?"

And without waiting for my reply, not even moving my perplexed, motionless hand from her breast, she added, "More men have touched me than everyone on this ship. But that's finished now, I want you to know. That's why I'm changing lands. And I would rather pass as a man, though I despise all such beings, than go on being a whore. That's all over and done with."

Repeating that last phrase, she now angrily removed my hand from her body and her clothing—as if I had put it there on my own in the first place!—and brusquely stepped away from my company with a glance full of an intense fury that consigned me to the category of the enemy, and joined a group who were killing time exchanging stares with one another, lacking any conversation to raise them out of the doldrums of their boredom, because there was no other place to accommodate them and they were tired of looking at the striations in the wood planks. Not for a moment did I remove my gaze from her; I did not know if she would want to trust everyone else with what she had used for wounding my hand—and up to that moment, only my hand—but which afterward would cut like a fatal illness through the rest of my body, my thoughts, my dreams, my appetite, my words . . . There was no worse place to find myself smitten by love, because there was absolutely nothing I could do for distraction!

On what remained of the voyage, and that was most of it, in fair weather or foul, I tried in every way to talk to her again, that loveliest of women dressed like a boy. But with equal obstinacy she took pains to avoid and ward off my gaze, and the most I could manage was that one day, only one other day, did she aim a few words in my direction, though it was not as if she were talking to me in particular; she spoke as if she were talking to someone who was not myself, to anyone at all, to the person I used to be and not this injured being whose whole body now bore the effect of that efficient weapon which her firm, gentle breast had become within me: "In the lands we are going to, I have heard it said that there is no 'yours' and 'mine' but that everything is 'ours.' And that no one asks, 'Who goes there?' and no doors are secured with locks and chains, because everyone is everyone's brother. I have heard this said. And the only rule is that of loyalty to the brothers. To be one of them you cannot be weak, a coward, a woman. But even though I am a woman, I will see if I can fit in with that kind of life, because that is the best life." Yet she did not look me in the eye while speaking to me; she talked so anyone could hear her, although this "anyone" happened to be me.

It was not difficult to find out how well she kept herself from confessing to anyone else that she was a woman, because from no one else did she try to keep herself apart, as she did me; while all the while Smeeks was wishing, it is true, to feel again the softness of her breast in the palm of his hand, the first breast of a woman he had ever touched, but also, or more especially, to be close to her, to be her friend and confidant once again, to be part of her, to hear her sweet voice, and— why not?—to find out what more there might be underneath her shabby, cheap, deceptive clothing, to ask her why she walked that way, so hesitant and uncertain, and if she did not want me to touch her I wouldn't do it, I would be just the way she wanted, but I would be *hers* . . . I imagined conversations I might have, or wished I could, with her, in one of which I heard myself saying, "I realize you are not a man, but that is not so important; I realize that, in spite of being a woman, you are just like everyone else, looking for a way to live far from cruelty and poverty," because I wanted to show my understanding in order to remain close to her. This imaginary conversation is one I recall very well because—oh, how the joke was on me, as time went on! Smeeks had no idea what awaited him! First the voyage: neither she nor the majority of the rest of us had ever set foot on the high seas, much less considered what it meant for both feet to spend more than thirty days constantly lurching and staggering beneath us! Moreover, the nausea of someone who never touches solid ground for six hundred hours is not conceivable within the word *nausea,* and no one knew what to call it when it took so long to finally put us down on dry land. And later on, that awful boredom into which the passengers were plunged, shut up in the cabin that smelled ten times as bad when the squalls were unleashed, as we will relate below . . .

But not for me; for throughout the entire voyage after this encounter, not a single moment of boredom touched me. Every one of those seconds, as if they were nooks and crannies in a desiccated body, was filled with the hope of having *her* nearby, *her* body, *her* eyes, *her* voice, infusing the time with the artful reality of my love through which *she* belonged exclusively to Smeeks, and thus avoiding the viscosity of that boredom into which everyone else seemed to be immersed. What was there about *her* that disturbed me so? My eyes saw nothing, my ears heard nothing that jumped out at them. The substance with which I charged every hour with another truth by using it to bombard every single one of its seconds spewed forth in a torrent from its center on the palm of this hand that I had touched her breast with, and at night, hopeless with love, I would knot my fists so forcefully that my fingernails bloodied my palms as I tried to stifle the flow of emotion that so tortured me and which I trusted had its cure in the possibility of satiety.

So many years now have I done nothing but make fun of that little boy so moved by the woman's flesh hidden in the darkness of the blouse of coarse fabric worn by the impoverished youth. It does not need saying that my heart was prodigal in spinning out the bizarre fabric of days shot through with the desire to touch again and again and again that small bit of flesh that I imagined as white, that I knew was infinitely sweet and impregnated with a fragrance unfamiliar to me, a woman's fragrance. And how did I know it was so gravid with that fragrance? Because in the palm of my enamored hand I had read that smell of her! Forty years would bring forth the laughter of ridicule over that boy so thrilled by a bit of flesh during an entire voyage, flesh that was for him alone, revealed and modestly held back in the same gesture—because there came a day on which I could have covered the sea encircling the globe with the skin of the flesh yielded to us in the brothels of Jamaica and Tortuga; and could have covered it twice over with the skin of the women who were taken by force, without my attaching any more value to it than that of a few coins (that always turned into nothing in our hands) and of my being a counterpart of the dream of violence that I was immersed in for thirty-seven years. And even now, something that resembles tenderness, when I see him in my mind's eye, moves me to laughter. . . .

The moment she made me the accomplice/enemy of her secret, the voyage changed for me, in the midst of my uncertain fears, the stench of the vomiting, and the invincible nausea that seemed to envelop all of us like a blanket of air and water, and it turned into the frame surrounding the stimulation embodied in that tiny patch of skin, soft and firm, miraculously arrested almost horizontally, which sometimes was my delight and sometimes a feverish torture. I was unable to contain myself and found myself forced to share my confinement with dozens of drowsing youths bewildered by this confinement

and battered by disillusionment; who among them had imagined this voyage would be so tedious? None at all, and even less
so the fact that the dangerous storm would represent nothing
but the obligation for them to remain locked up, no matter what
happened, in the hold/cabin; or that when we actually did run
into a pirate ship it would take flight the moment we measured
off against each other.

I wanted to touch her once more, even if it were only
once. . . . And for what purpose was I so eager to touch that
piece of flesh belonging to a woman who could not be mine,
since I did not know how to make any woman mine? And
moreover, the crowded conditions endured by us indentured
servants of the Company, bundled together like carrots in a sack
in the ship's hold close beside the supplies I already mentioned,
beside the cow that never stopped moaning, made us seem more
like things than persons in that place, more like ship's stores
than true believers. Despite the morning prayer, and that every
time the watch changed they had our voices join in more prayer,
we were as faithless as fava beans, huddled in that gloomy hold
which in no way resembled the aspirations, dreams, and de-
sires that made this unbearable voyage bearable; nor did the
awful storms and the slavery that awaited us in the new lands
without our being aware of it then. And under those conditions, what could a fava bean do—that is exactly what I was—
with a woman? Why weren't our prayers enough to make us
more human? What else was there to say when, at daybreak,
the cabin boy who announced the dawn, sang out,

Blessed be the light
    And the Holy Cross
And the Lord of Truth
    And the Holy Trinity;
Blessed be the soul
    And the Lord who leads us.
Blessed be the day,
    And the Lord who sends it.
God give us good day,
    May the ship have safe passage,
A good master, and worthy crew, AMEN!
    May they make this voyage safe.
God give you good morrow,
    Lords of stern and prow.

Was it necessary that we repeat or add something more as we joined in his song?

When I would see her pass by with that unusual step of hers and holding her dish—which was the time when she had the greatest leeway to move around—or when she would slyly brush against me as if not realizing that this body she was touching belonged to *me,* her confidant, the only one who knew her secret and hence for her the only man on the whole ship, since I was the only one who knew that she was a woman and the only one who, for her, would throw himself into the ocean headfirst and let it devour me in my despair over not being able to put my two palms (I was no longer content with one) on every part of her body, the only one who would throw himself headfirst and in vain, just for her, into the deep, endless, silent sea . . . In vain, because if I *was* the only man on the whole ship for her, then I was also the only being of whom she wished to know nothing at all ("That's all over and done with," she had said); her confiding had erased me completely from the map. On the other hand, the others did have some interest for her, or at least for the "him" they thought she was. Those who told her the sea stories in which we all dressed the silly, childish fears that awaken in the dark of night on the high seas made her open her eyes wide as if they might want to jump out of their accustomed place and leap completely away from her. And the ones who refused to show her the rudiments of even the simplest tasks necessary for the ship's navigation exerted still more attraction over her, from the cabin boys who pushed her away so she was unable to see how they handled the sheets that kept the sails in trim or how they bailed out the water taken on by the ship, to the old salts who moved their thick bodies into her line of vision so she could not watch them keeping the fire alive on the sand where they warmed the grim meals with which they tortured our palates at midday. . . . Every one of the crew or the novice cabin boys, all those who were going in search of adventure or in hopes of making a living, those who did not yet know why they were going, those who were sorry they had come, those who had more than once crossed the ocean sea as well as those who had never voyaged before, the ones who had begged on the streets or been sold by their families—every single one of them was more interesting to her than I was because I was the repository of a secret that bound me ardently to her. . . .

The restless memory of this episode that made me suffer so—because the sickness of love *is* suffering—is making me lose all sense of order. Better that I take it up again so as to be able to relate how the voyage continued:

First of all, it was necessary to flee from the English ships. Hard by the Isle d'Ornay were four frigates waiting to accost our fleet, and we were afraid not only of their despoiling us of our goods, arms, and supplies, but also of suffering their cruelty. While we were waiting for their attack, many stories were passed around describing the horrors perpetrated by the English pirates, to which in my imagination I added the perils my companion, being a woman, was exposed to, dangers that (in my imagination, again) I confronted valorously, saving her in a thousand ways, all different, all of them heroic, from the lust and violence of the English. Fortunately, some fog arose and prevented us from being seen and perhaps falling into their hands. Who would have said then that J. Smeeks would ever become a member of the crew of a ship of that sort! I would never have believed him, just as now I find it difficult to believe in the veneration I felt then toward my companion, the fidelity I maintained toward her skin.

Throughout the first part of the voyage we remained close to the French shore. The population along the coast, fearful and rather uneasy, saw us sailing by and took us for the English, unmindful that we shared their fear and that the reason we stayed where they could see us was to protect ourselves from the very men they feared. We ran up our flags but they put no trust in them, nor in that the hulls of our ships were painted in bright colors, nor that our sails were decorated with crosses and shields; in their fright they saw us only as the talons of the English marauders, seeking out a good place to show our strength and raid their towns. To find ourselves taken for the assailants laid the fires of ambition for at least some of my companions; holding their reeking bowls in their hands, they would devour the houses of the rich with their eyes and fantasize about sumptuous meals doubtless being prepared beneath those roofs by gorgeous women, singing all the while (women of exuberant breasts and blouses with plunging necklines)— meals that could well be cooking there just for them. . . .

The wind favoring us as far as Cape Finisterre, a huge storm came up that separated us from the other ships. For eight long days the storm threw the passengers from one side of the ship to the other, and for twenty-four hours a day the crew made enormous efforts to keep the ship under control. The first day, when the storm had not yet reached full force, the Captain, punishing a flagrant lack of discipline, forced a crewman to mount to a yardarm and remain up there without permitting him to be lashed to it, and into the sea he fell, totally exhausted. Throwing out a line, they rescued him from the frenzied waters; yet if his authority had so moved him, the Captain could have punished him with death.

As always when encountering such furious winds, they brought in all the sails, the hull being unable to bear the weight of those enormous masses of canvas standing full out against the wrathful gusts, after which the sailors trusted only to luck as to the ship's course. The carpenters and the caulkers had not a moment of repose, they were so busy fixing and over-hauling things everywhere, bailing water out of the craft several times a day, and not merely in the mornings as in good weather. No one was able to set foot on the plank thrust out over the ship's sides to give us a place where we could relieve ourselves, the pitching of the ship making it dangerous in the extreme, so the crew members would shit and piss right on the deck, and the passengers did likewise in the cabins we were stuffed into, alongside the messy gobs of vomit left there by those who did not know how to behave like seamen in a storm: for if they began to puke in a corner next to the other filth, they would end up smeared all over with it, so ensuring that whoever had not vomited before this would certainly vomit now. The cow, doubly lashed by each of its four legs, refused to drink water and in the midst of all the furor got so thin it was almost invisible, continually loosing a piteous mooing sound into the air that made it seem more like the ship's cat than a proper milk cow.

Those who were not throwing up every time they turned around would gnaw on hard biscuits and dried fish when fear did not prevent them from eating or, just as likely, an attack of nausea prompted by the nausea of others nearby. The sand clock had gotten damp and the hours went by unmarked because no one sang them out, nor were the chanteys heard that in good weather the chorus of sailors would bellow out while raising the sails.

> *Rise — my hearties*
> *God grant us — help*
> *we're here — to serve*
> *to keep — the faith*
> *the Christian — faith*
> *to flog — the pagans*
> *and spite — the Saracens.*

At night, with the storm clouds shutting us in, one could see nothing at all, and in no way did the glow of my love for *her* shed any light for me. So dark was the darkness that not even our hands were visible. We were even more afraid in that darkness when, with the storm abating somewhat, the rolling and pitching would seem to slacken, as if the ship were beginning a mournful dance of death. Totally blind on those blind nights, lacking both moon and stars, with the ship's lamp extinguished by the storm and the total darkness permitting our fancies to dwell on lands and beings that, so it was said, peopled the sea, we imagined ourselves approaching the islands of no return, we believed we were about to bump into fish as huge as islands, or phantom ships, all-engulfing waterspouts, enormous octopuses, fantastic amphibious beings whose bizarre tentacles would snatch sailors off the deck and take them down to the deep of the ocean. . . . Amid those wonders, those monsters, I saw myself rescuing *her*! . . . Those who managed to conquer their dread, despite their fear of navigating without the orientation of the stars, without sails, completely given over to the will of the tempest, would let their imaginations sail away to the marvelous islands of the Antilles, the Seven Cities, Saint Brendan's Isle, the Amazon, all of them filled with marvels and riches, and there were even those who wondered about the Fountain of Youth, believing it to be on the land closest to hand. . . . Our voices, never too loud, went back and forth through the hold without our being able to distinguish who brought up and described each marvel, each monster, and there was a moment when we all together (even I, so different from the others by reason of my attachment to *her*) formed something like a single body unembarrassed by its own excretions and above which the hours, closing in over it, hovered with a gray tone identical to *no* and *yes,* to *now* and *always* and *never.* . . .

The gale had held on for eight eternal days when the cow died. It seemed as though its death were sufficient to restore good weather. Without its continual moaning, the hours seemed to thaw out, and we returned to a situation in the hold that somewhat resembled the way it was in the beginning, when it had first received us with its greasy planks and the shameless rats jumping about here and there; and the temperature awakened, too, rising so high that it made life in the hold unbearable. . . . The old sailors in charge of the kitchen butchered the cow, with the help of the barber, the only one of the younger sailors not pressed into checking on the condition of the ship. Part of the animal was boiled in the cauldrons and part they salted down and put out in the sun to dry, but all of it, now silent and milkless, ended up in the bellies of the crew and the hungriest passengers.

Resuming our progress was not difficult, by dint of working the ship. Thanks to the fact that the tempest had never wakened to its whole fury, we had managed to keep our anchors, the tackle, the sails, and all the small boats.

The weather being fair as far as the Tropic of Cancer, it was very favorable to us from there on, which gave us much joy, since we were in dire need of water, so much so that we were now rationed to four gills a day. The thirst was even hurting our eyes; if the men had had any need of tears during this time in order to relieve their despair, as in the middle of the storm, they would have found none at all, their eyes being altogether dry from such thirst. On four gills a day and a diet of salt meat, how would even the little water necessary for shedding tears ever reach the eyes? Not a single drop of water did they get. . . .

And it was then that one of the strongest and most robust sailors took sick, his gums so swelled up it was impossible to see his teeth. The barber having bled them, a black liquid was all that came out. Once bled, the swelling went down, but in a few days the sailor was left without a tooth, not a single molar or eyetooth. He groaned aloud, at the top of his voice, "Four molars I used to have there, for in all my life I never had a tooth or grinder pulled nor has any fallen out or been eaten away by abscess or decay!"

His complaint merely concealed another that was more gloomy. He already knew the outcome of his illness, for he had the scurvy. Yet to come was the awful swelling of his limbs amid the most horrible pain, the barber bleeding them again and removing some fetid liquid, and then, inexorably, death.

Approaching Barbuda, an English corsair tried to give chase, but as soon as he saw he had no advantage over us, he drew off. We sought to give chase then ourselves, but unable to reach him, we returned to our course.

We passed within sight of Puerto Rico, a pleasant island garnished with leafy trees and underbrush right up to the peaks of its mountains. We also saw the island of Hispaniola and I understood, with panic and grief—even though I also longed for it—that we were on the verge of reaching our destination.

Thirty-five days after weighing anchor, on June 7, 1666, without having lost a man on the voyage (the man sick with scurvy and now toothless, with both arms swollen and bled, was yet alive), we dropped anchor off the island of Tortuga.

two

My arrival on the island of Tortuga was cloaked in a veil that clung wantonly to my body and my soul, numbing me to everything, and that I would do no wrong to call *disillusionment*. So hastily did they get those of us who were indentured to the Company on deck, and loaded down with bundles, like true ants, that there was no time to get an idea of the island from there, nothing could I see of the place to which I had come.

The moment we set foot on dry land, a foreman awaited who hurriedly divided us into fast-moving, orderly squads under the command of youths of our own age, although self-assured colonists of Tortuga already (or so they seemed to me then, but later on I realized that if they were doing work of that sort, it was only because they were so slow to catch on), who led us immediately to the places where we would sleep and eat: huge sheds that imitated the structures of the natives in having no paint or decoration, nor any furniture, and that benumbed my eyes like empty hulks of gloomy barrenness in which I was unable to see any alleviating quality, roasting me with a heat I thought inexplicable and that only with the passing of time would I accept as the natural temperature, though always unbearable and all the more accentuated by the anguish of not knowing where *she* had ended up (and which this kind of climate made all the worse), whether in some nearby shed or, something I sensed and feared, on some other island, a likelihood I was not long in substantiating because I did not see her anywhere. I was not certain then if I really wanted to have reached Tortuga or if I wanted the voyage never to end. I had been defending myself against the pains of love by seeing her, and the perfect picture of unhappiness consisted in seeing her no longer.

On the other hand, I still was not aware of the prohibition against women that she already knew about for certain: women could not live on Tortuga. Though daring enough to travel as a man, she did not appear ready to live forever behind a mask, which she had betrayed at least once during those thirty-five days with the confidence that I know she needed to divulge so that perhaps just one person in the whole immensity of the ocean would be aware that she was a woman; and thus it was impossible to think she would have been able to remain permanently hidden as a woman without needing to betray her intention if she stayed on the island.

At dawn the following day they took us to the fields to work: some of us to harvest coffee, tobacco, or cassava root, others to the packing sheds, to move things about, to work in the houses of the Company dignitaries. What fell to me in the way of harvesting tells me nothing; the assignment must have lasted only a few days, not enough to learn what the foreman tried by force to inflict on my body dulled by melancholy, by the seasickness that had as yet not gone away, and the weariness of spending my nights thinking of her, still enveloped by the veil mentioned a few lines back, the one I called *disillusionment,* but which the bizarre quality of the climate, always heavy with the sun that exacerbates the cruelty in the hearts of men, would turn into something else; because everything changes on Tortuga, so that it took me days to discover that if I avoided always being under the direct rays of the sun the heat became more bearable, months to learn so wisely to keep my eyelids half closed so the sun would not blind me, and years to discover the appropriate movements of my mind in order that Tortuga would not get away from me in its continual shifting from shape to shape, insistent and imprecise. The very features of the island were bizarre, jagged, like the songs I heard in the nights: rhythms that I never imagined existed, insane, crazy rhythms, black as the skin of those who unleashed them, and that made me feel ashamed in our first encounters, that I never wanted to listen to, and that, were it not the custom among the Brethren of the Coast not to forbid anything that might appeal to others even though their tastes were disagreeable or irritating to us, I would have said it was necessary to prohibit for the general well-being of our spirits and the growth of our minds. Because the sounds they produced with the palms of their hands and other parts of their bodies, and with skins

stretched over frames or wooden boxes, forever striking them
until producing the feverish image of what is only possible when
bodies are rubbing together in the black ceremony of the flesh,
cannot join with anything great or noble nor establish the basis
of any other world that is not that of an assault or the desper-
ateness that is so eager for an assault, as happened with us who
remained walled in by the violence with which we lived. . . .
But let us suppose we were able to prohibit such harmful
rhythms. Would we have been able to prohibit the climate and
the countenance of Tortuga? Because it was not only the music
that fermented our hearts and prepared our bodies, whetting
our thirst for raids, for violence and profligacy . . . We were
also influenced by the plentiful trees that, all over the rocky,
sheer terrain of the mountainous island, so abundant with crags,
sent out their roots over the rocks and entwined themselves
together without reentering the earth, bare and twisted together
like ivy branches against a wall; and by the steep cliffs pocked
with shallow grottoes which, along with the fringes of sand here
and there, ring the island. . . . The natural aspect of the island
is so peculiar that the translucent waters of those seas lose their
transparency as they approach the island, which makes me think
that the harshness of its climate perhaps must set them to boiling, since they add no refreshing quality to the burning air; just
as the exposed tree roots do not wish to bury themselves in the
rocks, as if it were the harshness of the climate that prevents
them from doing so, and therefore, giving the lie to their nature as roots, they prefer to remain out in the open, although

the air howls searingly all around them, rather than sink into the even more awful heat of the earth. Boiled, burned, cooked by its climate, Tortuga would make anyone change who comes near it.

In the ship on which I came, there were some soldiers, as I have mentioned before. They too had been engaged by the French West Indies Company, but for the purpose of wresting outstanding payments or the return of merchandise from the colonists on Tortuga who had refused to respect agreements with those they were opposed to because they were not of the same religion. The Company had taken possession of the island in 1662, arrogating the colony for itself, with its own commissaries and its own servants, and ordering the residents of the island to buy all their supplies from the Company, first having ingratiated itself with the colonists by announcing that purchases would be made on credit. But it was one thing for the Company to impose itself, and quite another for it to operate that way.

The farmers were the first ones against whom the soldiers determined to move, they being the easiest victims. It was le Turque who was chosen; they flattened his house and carried off anything of value, they beat him when he tried to stop them, and, letting their horses run loose over his tobacco fields at a time when the plants were scarcely out of the ground, they reduced his plantings to mud and upthrown seedlings, thinking thus to intimidate the others and obtain what was owed them, the only reason for their being on Tortuga; after which they returned to the ship then anchored before Cayonne, following the orders of the governor established by the Company in the foolish belief that he was putting them safe from possible attacks by the colonists. The following morning, they found the night guard murdered, his mouth and ears and belly split open and filled with earth taken from the fields belonging to le Turque and a message written on the deck in the blood from his mutilated limbs, which had been used one after the other as paintbrushes, nearly worn to shreds from having been rubbed over the planks: YOU ARE CATTLE, LIKE CATTLE YOU WILL ALL EAT GRASS. The trail of blood from the body underlined the sentence and ran down to the ship's railings and scuppers, as if the body were a fountain of blood. The Captain having called everyone on deck, they were abruptly boarded by ferocious Brethren of the Coast who had reached the ship in canoes carrying a good deal of fodder for the soldiers, who, surrendering, were then forced to eat the plantings trampled into le Turque's fields, mingled with mud, shit, and weeds, an ingestion that killed more than one of them and and put the others into horrible pain for days altogether, after which they abandoned Tortuga, and because of which the commissaries put into effect the order that the *Saint Jean* had also brought them, which was that if they could not collect what was owed them or enforce the return of goods, they should sell whatever they had under their control, properties, merchandise, and indentured servants alike; a decision, which, as it included the almost absolute retreat of the Company, put jubilation into the hearts of the colonist farmers, who wasted no time in taking over the goods, quibbling over prices that were actually not assessed dearly by the commissaries, some out of a mixture of respect, fear, and admiration, the others simply out of hatred for the Brethren of the Coast, who were by all odds the winners in this business.

Joy was the feeling that went the rounds on Tortuga during those days, but not for me, because I was acquired, for my bad fortune and worse luck, by the most tyrannical and perfidious man ever roasted beneath Tortuga's sun, the Governor or Lieutenant General of that spot, set up by the Company itself. The words "joy" and "freedom" were circulating on Tortuga because the Brethren of the Coast claimed they owed loyalty only to God and the sea, but there was no freedom for me because I did not have a penny or anyone I could ask to pay off the price my cruel master demanded to give me freedom and my immunity: three hundred pieces of eight. His treatment of me was unbearable and it was impossible to escape.

There were slaves who had already tried it, either from him or from other masters who were just as cruel. I saw them strung up, hanged, exposed to the sight of all until the worms and the birds had left no more of them than their bones. Then bits of them fell to the ground in a jumble. The punishment that others received for their attempt was to have a leg cut off, and such legless slaves came to be so numerous that a French colonist on Martinique invented a way to make his slaves secure by a kind of imitation of those who were already missing a leg, with a short chain fastened at one end to an iron collar and at the other to one ankle, encircled in iron like the neck. So that some slaves, even though in possession of both their legs, hobbled around as if they had only one, with added injuries caused by the infernal heat, aggravated by the sun, that condensed on the metal collar and the ring that went around their ankle.

One slave who escaped was caught in the forest. His master had him tied to a tree, where he beat him on the back with sticks and bathed him in so much blood that it was running on the ground. Then the master had his wounds dressed with bitter lime juice mixed with salt and ground pepper, leaving him tied to the tree in that state for twenty-four hours, and repeating the torture later, until from being beaten and so badly mistreated the slave died, not without first screaming out, in a sharp, piercing voice that seemed to reach beyond the forest and lose itself in the sea, "May the powerful God of the Heavens and earth permit the devil to torment you as much before your death as you have done me before mine!"

Three or four days later, the evil spirit fell on that landowner. His own hands were his executioners, as he beat himself and scratched his own face so severely that it lost its shape, and he died in a pool of his own blood, like his slave, intensifying his torment with the salt and pepper of a punishment he never expected; the usual thing being that the landowners did whatever their ill will desired, and they could offer their slaves, no matter what their race, any maltreatment whatsoever, even death, because they were not within anyone's jurisdiction. Thus, for the slaves (Nau aside, for he was always out of the ordinary) the only possible escape, if they could not stick it out for the period of their indenture, being three years for the French and seven for the English, was death. The white slaves (black slaves and those who are a mixture of blacks and Indians, called *matates,* are not forced to work as hard as the Europeans, the landowners saying that the former should be taken care of since they belong to them forever, while the whites, on the other hand, who cares about them! they only have their services for three years), some sooner and others later, would fall into a certain sickness called *mal d'estomac* there, which is a total privation of all the senses and comes from their maltreatment and the change from the air of their natal land into something completely the opposite. If, as everyone knows, people die of sadness, of disillusionment, of the state of mind caused by deception in love, why should the French slaves not die under such cruel treatment in lands so different from those they are used to? They did not hear, they did not see, they did not feel the intense heat, nothing pained them, they suffered neither hunger nor thirst: before dying they entered into the realm of the stones.

I was not the only slave of the governor, but I was the only white one, so that, for the reasons just stated, the worst part fell to me, the hardest labor. My condition was not so strong as to be able to resist it, being as yet unused to Tortuga, because of the state of my convalescent heart and because my body, tortured by hunger, was still growing—as my nature, perhaps touched by Tortuga, dictated: hastily and excessively (in a short time having made me a tall man, unusually thin, but a man and no longer a boy, to whom *she* would not dare confess her secret now as she had done to my small, child's body). Several times I was on the verge of breaking down under the beatings and the harshness of my master, and doubtless I would have done so had it not been for two consolations: my new living quarters, less strange, barren, and severe, a stone building that formed part of the island's fort; and second, though of much greater importance, my relationship with the man who occupied the room next to mine, le Nègre Miel, who, though half blind, took me in without caring that I was a white Frenchman, finding me merely a young man tormented by a cruel master. Such compassion did I awaken in le Nègre Miel as he showed affection and generosity, bequeathing me his wisdom on the one hand and eternity on the other, through my account of his reminiscences and thoughts, which I will offer very shortly. My ability to substitute lies for work also provided no small aid for my survival, although for every ten lies I came up with, my master would catch me out in one, and then he really made me pay for it with his whip.

I wish to yield the right to speak to this man, to le Nègre Miel, just as I heard him tell his story more than once as he was healing my back injured by the beatings, furtively giving me extra portions of food, smoked meat, cassava bread, fruits, and plants that he was familiar with on Tortuga (to which, perhaps, I owe my unusual height), or restoring my wasted limbs with concoctions he brewed and administered, and that he taught me how to prepare and prescribe, during time snatched from my labors, behind my master's back, with the help of my clever lies:

le nègre miel's tale

I was born where the earth reaches its perfection. The climate is perfect: neither heat nor cold offers any reason to cover the body because the air itself clothes the skin exquisitely. There are wonders and an abundance of fruits, and the plants without exception are edible from flower to root, seeds, stems, leaves, branches and all. Water runs everywhere in cool branches, like that here in Tortuga which flows ceaselessly inside the fort, crossing the land here and there, so that no one ever suffers thirst and the earth is always covered with green. Zebras, lions, giraffes, elephants, antelopes: these are some of the wondrous animals, as varied as the fruits of the land, that populate the perfect valley in which I was born. Since I was very little, my father, my mother, and their brothers would teach me the secrets of nature, which spirits are hidden in which forms, and how to invoke them in order to cure diseases, heal wounds, make sadness depart. I also learned French, and even how to write it, because my mother's brother lived in a French city for several years. When it was time to cease being a child, I was initiated into virility. Then I learned greater secrets. A new initiation, which we called "Entering the World," took place when I was eighteen. In it, they sewed to my chest, transversally, from my left shoulder to the ribs on my right, the sash of leather and fabric that identifies those of us who come from that place where nature reaches its perfection; the rite being concluded, I left my own land, in the belief that I would return, as all my people had done before me, and without imagining that I would be plucked out of my beloved valley forever. That is why le Nègre Miel no longer sees. He prefers his sight to concern itself with memories, with what his eyes would not see were they to be opened. That is why le Nègre Miel always uses French when he speaks out loud. We should preserve by our silence the languages that our parents taught us, so they do not become wasted, so that in silence they can take pains deep within us to keep our spirits focused on high, and thus the gods will not ignore us and instead will protect us. The first village I served got into a bloody struggle with another village nearby. I will not give an account of the battles, to which my blood is so opposed, my time being spent healing wounds, curing the sick, strengthening people's broken health; thinking, when I was alone, that when seventy full moons had come and gone I would return to my own people, to the valley where all is perfection, to teach the children what had been taught to me plus what I had learned during the seventy moons, and to start a new line of descendants with someone of my own blood.

The conflict grew worse and the people of the village where I lodged were vanquished; together with the other young men, notwithstanding my lineage, I was taken prisoner in token of the defeat. I thought I would quickly find myself free, distinguished as I was by the sash that crossed my chest, in which everyone knew that I kept remedies useful for all. What I never imagined was that I would fall into the hands of the English, sold like the rest of us by the victorious village that acted as if I were one of the barbarians. Buried in the hold of a ship to make the voyage, I discovered I was going to places whose existence I had never suspected, without any of us in that cesspool being able to see where we were being taken, like merchandise, fastened with chains at the neck, the ankles, the wrists; roasting us, as we begged for cool air or at least for an end to the rocking back and forth. The ship we were traveling on was taken by French pirates and they quickly set sail for the Antilles. Such attacks on slave ships are not uncommon, but among these freebooters it was not customary and even inspired repugnance; but now needing resources to get ready for an ambitious enterprise in the Caribbean, they kept both ships, which was most unusual for them, the one in which they were sailing plus the one they had boarded, and set out immediately for the sale of their lucrative though disgusting booty.

When they came down below to take a look at us and I heard them speak amongst themselves, I made sure my correct French was noticed, but the only thing I obtained was a cold look at my chains, though not at my body; the one who vouchsafed this confirming only that the blacks were well secured and making his whip sound very close, almost touching me and actually hurting the one who was right next to me even though he was not connected to the same chain, an old man who spent all his time weeping, crying out his misfortune aloud, weeping for his sons and grandsons and complaining that his age had not been respected; and with good reason, since later, when on the open sea they brought us up on deck to choose and put a price on us, him they threw overboard thinking it unreasonable to waste food on him as being so old that no one would pay much for him, first cutting off his hands, his feet, and his head, in that order, to avoid having to remake the chain that linked him together with six others or else having to return his flesh to the hold to rot.

When it came my turn to go up on deck, I had a stroke of luck that was worth my life on Tortuga. They brought us up seven at a time because that was how many my chain joined together at the neck, wrists, and ankles; and all of us blinded by the sun that never came into the hold where they kept us entombed, into which a little light filtered only when they pulled back the hatch to lower our food and let in those who were to pour it into the feeding troughs. With the English it would be five men armed to the teeth (they being cowards, since we were fastened down so harmlessly, like nails in a wall) who amused themselves sometimes by leaving it out of anyone's reach; and now it was a single Frenchman who with cold patience arranged the food near our faces in the wooden troughs, we eating more like cattle than persons, being unable to use our chained hands to bring the food up to our mouths. I recovered from the dazzling sunlight sooner than the other six, or at least one of them, because I was able to see when we fell as one of us stumbled, still blinded by the sunlight, and we being joined by the same chain, all seven of us tumbled to the deck. Before my eyes was a leather boot, cut open at the toe with a knife so as not to irritate a wound that did not wish to heal, and I knew immediately that this was not a wound

caused by a weapon or a knife but a vein that was
sick, that had burst below the skin, and so I said as
much, out loud and in French while facedown on
the deck, adding that I knew how to cure it with
the remedies in the pouches of the sash on my
chest. The man with the boot, second in command
of the expedition and commander of the slave ship,
because the Captain was in the pirates' ship, gave
the order for them to release me from the chain
of seven to which I was soldered, and ordered the
blacksmith brought over from the other ship to get
me free. Noticing that there was a delay, I said it
was not necessary to free me in order to cure him
because healing wounds, causing illnesses to go
away, and curing melancholy was in my blood and
that if His Excellency the one with the opened boot
would permit all seven of us to draw near him, I
being unable to move without the other six, I would
begin to cure him immediately and with great pleasure. He gave the order for us to approach. All
seven of us sank down to examine the wound.
Some of them were squeezed closer than the others for the chain to permit my hands to take from
my sash a powder of dried herbs that removes pain
if rubbed over the wound while being blown on
with a warm breath. Again all seven of us bent down
before his boot, and even farther down, with our

heads almost on the deck so I could apply the powder. Then we stood up to allow cool air to reach the empowdered wound and I asked for honey, or sugar if they had no honey. There was some honey aboard the other ship. It arrived together with the blacksmith, packed in a huge barrel because I had not said that I needed only a little of it. Even before they began to strike at the chain in order to free me, I applied some honey to the wound (which, from that moment, because of the deceptive powder, already showed some relief) and repeated the application on succeeding days, until with the passing of seven of them it closed over completely. Now without the chain about my neck, I put my hand to the remedies I had brought with me, relieving one man from a hopeless migraine, getting rid of bothersome lice on those who allowed a seed from my country to be placed in their right ears, and aches and pains of all kinds from all who suffered from them; remedies that brought me some prestige, so that when we reached Cuba to exchange the contraband slaves for powder and arms from the Spaniard with whom they had already arranged the business, I had already been admitted into the Society of the Brethren of the Coast, swearing fidelity to them, abandoning the name given me by my parents for that of le Nègre

Miel, and checking over the contract they gave me
to sign and on which I printed my new name with
a clear hand, to the great surprise and rejoicing of
the other Brothers, who had not believed it possible for a black man to be able to read and write.
Because of this, and also for knowing how to cure,
I did not come into the Society as a matelot, or
sailor, nor did I need a master or anyone whose
clothes I would have to wash, make his meals, clean
his hut, cultivate his garden, or remain by his side
during combat and protect him for two years like
any other aspirant for registration on Tortuga; although what is certainly true is that they made my
membership in the Society conditional on the ap-
proval of the Council of Older Pirates, before
whom, upon my arrival, I swore my loyalty before
the cross and on a Bible, as if I were both a Catho-
lic and a Protestant at once, and I wrote the sentence they dictated so it could be seen that my hand
was skilled in lettering. When we arrived at
Tortuga, while everyone else was preparing for the
expedition, I wandered around over a large part
of the island and even went over by canoe to La
Grande Terre on Hispaniola looking for materials
to replenish my remedies, of which I found more
than I expected, rejoicing me in the extreme, but
I felt that the spirits on Tortuga were so powerful

that I obtained a dog to go with me and warn and protect me by being close by, and in that way I was able to conquer my fear.

Before I had time to think twice about it, we weighed anchor with our Admiral. I have already told you how alien fighting is to my blood. You will understand how repelled I was when you know how the freebooters behave, because they are so ferocious in their assaults, so cruel to those they have conquered, and also merciless with the weak. It was my good luck that that first expedition was extraordinary, Smeeks, extraordinary! It was not after the first attack that I decided never to sign another contract, but only after observing their cruelties and how they love to make the blood flow. But I admire the pirates. They are noble, they are loyal . . .

I accepted everything as if I had gotten the drift of it, even though I did not understand a word, but with those conversations, for which we snatched the time from my master (if he found out he would get back at me by whipping me for the work I had not done or the work I had put into deceiving him, or for my exhaustion and dullness from having stayed up the whole night long with eyes wide open, listening to le Nègre Miel, paying attention to his secrets and his skills instead of sleeping and resting in order to have the strength for the fearful work-days the Lieutenant General of the island forced on me), I gradually learned not only to recognize the medicinal herbs (to see, in his terms, the "spirit" in them) and how to prepare them and apply them and to what ailment or mood, but also who the pirates were, the way the Brethren of the Coast were organized, their Society, and, through his chatting, to love those terms I had never thought about before this—"freedom," "equality": the pillars of the Society. He told me about Tortuga and I was learning fascination for the island, thinking, in a dim but somehow correct fashion, that Tortuga remained at some distance from me, le Nègre Miel being my only connection with such a spot, a place where I would like to go and from which the beatings and cruelties of my master continually tore me away.

Le Nègre Miel told me the details of his first participation in a pirate raid, for it was not, as he himself said, violent by nature, but rather more like that of Hawkins, a pirate who, hating the blood but lusting after the winnings, would deceive and beguile; who on more than one occasion found from among his victims themselves the purchasers of goods he had recently seized. A band of freebooters with le Nègre Miel disembarked in the area around Campeche and waited in concealment, a little inland, for the passage of a group of Spaniards whom they subdued by force of blows, removing their clothing and tying them up with all manner of knots and ropes, and gagging them so cleverly that it took some time to remove the gags; they then dressed in their clothing and imitated their procession (something which amused le Nègre Miel greatly, he himself being dressed as a Spaniard, though an impossible one) as they hastily turned their steps toward the town square, where they began to raise a great fuss, pretending to be afraid, shouting out in the excellent Spanish of freebooters French and English, "The pirates are coming! Pirates are attacking! Pirates!" which of course was the truth, because they pointed back along the path where they themselves had just done the attacking, while le Nègre Miel, that no one would see his black face, covered it with his hands wrapped in bandages, screaming as if the devil were pecking at his eyes, pretending to have a wound that he didn't have . . . nor would ever have, because all the well-armed men sallied out quickly in the direction shown to them, a little inland, while the rest of the pirate ships, receiving the signal agreed upon, sailed into the bay, took charge of the fortress, subdued the town, and closed off the entrance to the place with such a strong force that le Nègre Miel never heard a single burst of gunpowder; meanwhile the armed citizens of the town hastened toward Champotón for reinforcements, realizing they were too few to confront the pirates. The latter meanwhile hastily plundered the church, seized all the dyewood (called *palo de Campeche* by the Spaniards) piled up in a warehouse, along with several loads of cassava flour and a little gold they had managed to squeeze from the most pusillanimous of the rich, and, quite happy to have gotten their booty without any greater effort, went back to their boats just as the citizens came up with so many reinforcements that in any case it would have been impossible to vanquish them.

On the deck of the subjugated slave ship le Nègre Miel had seen more blood while freeing from his chains the old man who was mutilated then thrown into the ocean than in the assault on Campeche, but on the other hand, his second and last expedition was not one he wanted to tell me about, claiming that there were things it was better not to repeat and that nevertheless I would see enough of it if I stayed on Tortuga, because even though he had not taken part in other expeditions, he could cover the island with ink, if it were made of paper, from the tales of atrocities and violence by the Brothers in pursuit of their booty. And all for what?—le Nègre Miel always added—since the Brothers, like the good folk they were, well knew that their spoils were not worth anything at all, for they would squander them in less time than it took him to tell me about it, all on excesses that a boy of my age ought not to hear about.

Other things there were that he did not want to mention in front of me, either. One of them, had he done so earlier, would have saved me a great deal of embarrassment and the women of The House in Port Royal some annoyance, but the only reference he ever made to brothels was not in that sense, and even that one slipped out only in his final words to me. Because le Nègre Miel sickened suddenly (or he appeared to become ill), and, refusing to accept his own medicines, he wasted away rapidly before my very eyes, to my great grief and despair, claiming that his hour had come, without explaining to me why until the last moment, when he said to me, "I am going away now. I know that I should make you flee with the pirates and not leave you in the hands of someone who does not follow the Law of the Coast. But I am not abandoning you,

Smeeks. My death is not natural. For the poison I was given, there is no remedy. My line will be cut off. I will not sow the earth with another of my blood. I gave no one the blood of consciousness, but you I have shown everything that one can learn. Le Nègre Miel asks you, this is his last wish, that you remember him always, so that my stay in the darkness of the earth is not altogether a desolation. Through your memories, what your eyes have seen will have entry to the darkness of my life, and after you die, what your children see and the children of your children; because you will speak to them about le Nègre Miel and they will remember me without having known me, as I remember my parents, the parents of my parents, and even their grandparents. Bequeath your lineage to me, for I squandered my seed among the Brethren and in the brothels of Port Royal, without ever thinking about the approach of my death! And respect the Law of the Coast above every other law!"

I tried to give him some serenity with a thousand and one words and demonstrations of affection born from the deepest sincerity. And I swore him an oath to which I am still faithful and which allows me to narrate my story to you: *I will remember you always, and when I have children I will tell them about you, and they to their children, but if I have no descendants, I promise you, le Nègre Miel, that I will conquer death in the name of your memory, and that I myself, with these eyes that are watching you die, these ears that are listening to you, and this heart that loves you, will remember you always.*

three

I t is easy to guess, without my saying it, the pain and desolation that le Nègre Miel's death caused me, believing as
I did that with him I had lost the capacity to survive. My
strength flagged, the debility brought on by my master's beatings renewed itself, I fell ill. What I was not long in realizing
was that it was not unfounded, that pronouncement of le Nègre
Miel's, *I am not abandoning you, Smeeks.* No, not even in death
did he abandon me. The illness brought on by my grief over
his disappearance made my master decide to sell me to avoid
losing the money he had put out to acquire me, as if he would
not recoup it with interest now; having purchased me so cheaply
from the Company, he yet sold me only half alive for more,
though not nearly as much as I would have brought were I
healthy, or at least not sick. My condition was feeble, and certain am I that no one but Pineau would have thrown away his
money to acquire me, the noble and generous Pineau, who
spent seventy pieces of eight on one who was more dead than
alive.

It took me no longer than the time it cost to get well again under the faithful care of my new master to learn that Pineau wanted me to know that he was an enemy of the enslavement of whites, blacks, or *matates,* considering it a barbaric outrage to traffic in persons as if one were dealing with things, that being opposed as he was to the business of "thine" and "mine," he deplored doubly that anyone would think himself the owner of any person, that he had paid the Lieutenant General of the island the money agreed upon for me not in order to be Smeeks's owner but because of le Nègre Miel; and when I asked him why because of le Nègre Miel, he answered that as I was still very young, he should not tell me any more. When I insisted, he said he had spent a decade trying to get le Nègre Miel to share his knowledge with him, that he had offered him, first, his interest, which was no small thing because Pineau was the most highly regarded surgeon on the island and the only one who had been so before, in Europe; and then later on, to exchange knowledge each with the other, to which le Nègre Miel had answered, *Forget it, Pineau; I am not a butcher, I do not wish to learn about your scissors and your knife, I do not like to speak with those things.* Nor had he offered him gold or money, knowing that besides being useless it would just make le Nègre Miel angry at him, yet he did offer him any object falling into his hands that he thought might appeal to him, like the vessel le Nègre Miel had given me when he died, a piece of fine Bohemian glass showing a hunter with a belt from which dangled his prey: white, brown, and gray rabbits, and amongst them, in the same position, was also a woman looking at him (at the hunter), naked as the rabbits, while the proud, arrogant man clutched a sword in one hand and a gun in the other, yet wearing a gentleman's dress, with a plumed hat and fine hose, all done in bright colors and bearing a brace of inscriptions, which le Nègre Miel asked me about one day.

"Here, you can see, you can read and write. Read what it says there."

"I can't read it."

"Why can't you?"

"Because it's in a language that I scarcely understand."

"The same happened to me with that thing—when I took it in my hands and heard Pineau's description I realized it was something I scarcely understood; and why was he carrying the woman there? Because of her the hunter would have to move more slowly."

In exchange for myself, I thought, though I am not a piece of fine glass from Bohemia, as Pineau certainly is, le Nègre Miel had presented me with all his knowledge, and thus Pineau purchased me and became my salvation because I was le Nègre Miel's written book. In time I would discover that there was still another sort of link between him and le Nègre Miel and that although perhaps this African wisdom did interest him he was never going to set his hand to it, and that he had acquired me for a different reason than the one he confessed to.

Pineau was not the only one who knew of my connection with le Nègre Miel. As soon as I had recovered from my illness, it being nothing more than grief and debility but would yet have killed me had Pineau not appeared in my life, a messenger arrived with a letter for Pineau. When he had finished reading it, he said, "Let us go, and take all your medicines along," and we left for Jamaica, an island I was unfamiliar with.

The route to Jamaica seemed exceptionally beautiful to me then, because it was the first time that I saw the course that led away from Tortuga, the Basse Terre beach where Cayonne is situated, the bay formed by the coral barrier, perhaps two hundred meters wide, with the channel winding amongst the submerged coral through which one must enter and depart with great caution and skill, and the color of the sea, which, the more distant we got from the coral reefs surrounding Tortuga, the more prodigiously translucent it became, as it is, I found out later, throughout the greater part of the Caribbean. From a distance the peculiar geography of Tortuga became more evident: mountainous and craggy, with a great deal of exuberant vegetation, steep, rocky terrain, and huge cliffs, about forty kilometers long and eight across through its broadest part, rather small in comparison with the enormous islands around it. We went around Tortuga and Saint-Domingue (only seven kilometers separate them), La Grande Terre that used to be so abundant in wild cattle, which had reproduced prodigally because of the climate, multiplying by many times the stock brought by the first colonists, those wild beasts that had made possible, according to what Pineau gradually explained to me that day, the plentiful hunting by the buccaneers and which the Spanish, in order to rid themselves of the latter, had sought to exterminate and almost managed to do so, leaving so few animals alive that the buccaneers had been pushed into the sea for their food. By killing the animals, the Spanish had created their worst enemies.

"And now there are no cattle left?"

"A few, enough so that here and there a party of clever buccaneers can survive, but it is not easy for the colonists to hunt them, since because of the harassment the animals are forced to take refuge in the forest."

"Like the wild pigs on Tortuga."

"Exactly."

"Pineau, I helped to poison the dogs."

"You did? Wait till we return to Tortuga to see something that will make you understand the business about the dogs a little better."

And we changed the subject, without getting back to the dogs. But on our return to Tortuga, he came through with what he had said. Walking in a northerly direction, he took me to an enormous pit, perhaps thirty meters deep and fifty in diameter, called by some the Grottoes of the Plain. We got down into it by uncoiling ropes and taking advantage of the roots and branches of the trees breaching the walls. When we reached the bottom, the pit broadened out to form a gallery with high ceilings covered with stalactites. There lay what Pineau had come to show me: some still with their long hair and the remains of their clothing (skirts for the women, the men only with embroidered belts), dozens of skeletons of Carib Indians, lacking any trace of flesh, Indians who, according to Pineau, had hidden in the caves while fleeing and preferred to remain there and die of hunger and thirst rather than stubbornly to go out and be killed. When the colonists had exterminated the whole of the aboriginal population, they simply let the dogs go loose that they had brought from Europe, to avoid having to feed them, and these then reproduced so intensely that they managed to nearly eliminate the wild pigs in the forests of Tortuga, so that the Governor had some poison brought from France, and as I already knew, since I had done this with my own hands, ordered some horses to be sliced open from end to end and the poison inserted inside them so the dogs would be poisoned by eating them. They died by the hundreds from that stratagem, but not enough to eradicate them altogether, as was D'Ogeron's intention, and they continued to plague the natural hunting on the island.

When we arrived on Jamaica, the messenger urged us to hurry through the streets of Port Royal. I had never seen a richer city nor one that was decked out in as gaudy a way, with colorful houses of stone and wood, flowers appearing here and there, fountains and gardens and rotundas, so different from the muddy streets and gray buildings of my natal city, or the meager, plain wood buildings on Tortuga. It seemed ready for a festival, Port Royal did, and women wandered along the paved streets, laughing shamelessly, all dressed up in fine fabrics, hats, stockings of which their short dresses coquettishly allowed glimpses . . . For a youth such as I, brought up in poverty and slavery, Jamaica seemed like Babylon in all its glory, and its lovely women like spirits of joyfulness and well-being. So that the messenger kept pulling at us to hurry us along, and my head kept twisting back so that we might remain there, as my eyes were simply starting out of my head with all that color, those low necklines, the flowers and brightly painted façades, those ankles bare or else scarcely concealed under thin stockings . . .

Finally we arrived at our destination. It was perhaps the most imposing building in all of Port Royal, high as a church, surrounded by a lovely and very carefully tended garden, filled with flowers, peacocks, pheasants, and ducks, with ponds where small swans were swimming, their heads and necks being completely black and a white streak over their eyes. What was this palace to which we had been brought? We did not use the principal entrance; instead we went around the building along its left side, from where we could see a deep fosse in which an enormous beast lay inert beneath the sun's rays, flattened out like a serpent but with jaws like those of a wolf, which was called an "alligator," so I was told, and this one in particular was the "temple alligator," because it seemed placed there to guard the one that adorned this side of the garden with its also vivid colors, astonishing in a shrine so reminiscent of Rome.

By the door on the left side we entered a hall (I did not know yet that this was a "little drawing-room" of The House) very richly furnished, with curtains and fine tapestries, a chandelier above the center of the room, a lacquered table . . . I had not yet managed to take it all in when Madame entered. How I regret, even now, having spent the whole journey and the entire time since my arrival without asking what I had been called for! My character is always like that: I lend my attention to what I should not, entertaining myself with the details and allowing the most important thing to get by me unnoticed; staring at the little things, in disregard of the whole to which they belong. . . .

Madame asked to speak with me alone, and Pineau and the messenger left the room.

"It's happened to us again, once more at the full moon, everyone at once, and I have had to"— and here she broke into tears —"close The House because none of us can work. Besides, it makes everyone start crying and fighting with each other, because there is no one who is not susceptible, now that we've all got the Red Flag up. And now there is no le Nègre Miel to help us. . . . Just think! If it happened to us this month, next month it will do the same, and the next month, and the next . . . And if they all come back"—she had not ceased weeping, she was really upset—"if they get here with all their loot on days like this, we'll lose everything! All of us! It will be our ruin! Do what le Nègre Miel did, I beg of you! They say he taught you everything. . . . Change our days, so that some get it one day and others on another, like that! That accursed full moon! Get us out of this rhythm, because if it falls on the full moon, as le Nègre Miel knew only too well, it brings us pain, inflammations, and shattered nerves. . . . And we can't have it! The servants are never done washing the sheets, and the water in the pool out back looks like a river of blood! Look!"

She took me by the hand and we left the room, going toward the inside patio. I was unable to get over my confusion. I did not know what she was talking about, I did not understand a thing, and she gave me no time to think because she was now talking about something else, telling me about her life when she was the French painter's mistress. What "river of blood"? I was thinking, when I saw it before my own eyes, the black slaves rubbing huge, bloodstained sheets on the washing rocks, everything permeated with an odor that I was already familiar with, without recalling where it came from long ago, when I was a child. . . . She would not let go of my hand nor did she stop talking: ". . . If you didn't bring enough medications, come back before the weeks go by, please, and you can take it out in trade with whomever you choose here, with me if you like, anyone you prefer, and you can come any time you wish, as le Nègre Miel always did . . . always, that is, until he became acquainted with you, because then he was no longer faithful to us . . ." I was not resisting, or else my dullness did not resist the need to show itself, because I might at least have been able to close my mouth; and even though the sight of such a river of blood kept my feet glued to the floor, I having had no dealings with blood before this, I could have let myself be drawn along without opening my mouth; yet said I, "Who did this to them? Where are the wounds?"

"What wounds?"

"The ones with all the blood."

Madame gently brought me back into The House; she was also bewildered now and, without attempting to calm me in my fussing, made me climb the stairs. I do not know exactly when I became quieted down, but my voice seemed to have aroused the whole house. We were all in an immense bedroom and they surrounded me there, passing along from one to the next, in whispers, the phrase that defined me, "He's that friend of le Nègre Miel"; most of them were in their undergarments and their hair unfastened, as if it were midnight when it was actually midday, until, after beginning with my stupid questions once more ("Who's been hurt? Where are the injuries? Why call on me? Let us get someone with weapons to . . ."), Madame, who had brought me upstairs, screamed out: "This fellow doesn't know *any*thing!" half in fury and half hysterical, and some of the others broke out in laughter, others began to cry, and some simply turned away, when a girl of about my own age with deep rings under her eyes brought her face close to mine and asked, "You really don't know?"

"Know what?"

"About the Red Flag. Didn't le Nègre Miel tell you what to do about it?"

I said "no" by shaking my head, and the ones who were left in the room began to ask each other, "Could he have told him about it under a different name?"

"Ask him."

"Hey, you, what do you call this curse we get every month?"

I did not understand a thing and I did not know what to do, being partly ashamed and partly humiliated, on the verge of tears, when Isabelle came in, all made up and dressed for a party, huge and blond, and asked, "Is this him?" as if there were another man in the room with whom I might be confused. She came closer but still kept her distance and would not sit down, as if I were somehow disgusting; not even looking me in the eye, she introduced herself and explained, "I am the one le

Nègre Miel usually slept with, if he didn't feel like having someone else. What we need is for you to bring us some *l'herbe folle*.
Are you familiar with that herb?"

I nodded in assent, still unable to speak.

"Do you know how to prepare it?"

I nodded again.

"Go back to your island, find that herb, prepare it, and
give it to us spaced out, the way he used to do so we don't all
get this thing at the same time. And while you're at it, look for
someone to help you get over being such a blockhead!"

She turned half around to go out. Before leaving the
bedroom she turned her head and added, with a coquettish
wink, losing the imperative tone from her voice, "If you don't
find anyone there to help you out, don't worry. When you come
back we'll explain everything."

I did return, of course, as soon as I had the medicine
prepared. Isabelle took it on herself to explain to me what a
woman's body is like. I will not say that this was all to my pleasure. I had to do what up until then had only been done to me;
I discovered this when Isabelle swiftly ran her hands around
inside my clothing and settled my own bewildered hands com-
fortably on her back and especially her breasts, provoking a
trembling in me that was radically different from the one which
another breast had brought about in my palm; and so very radically different was it that in some obscure way it was the same.
An erection came on, the which having happened to me previously only when I was alone, and without my desiring it I found
myself inside her body. I moved my loins the same way le Nègre

Miel had moved his against me, and I was unable to avoid thinking of him and breaking out in tears at the same time my perplexed penis burst out inside Isabelle. No, it was not pleasant.
I felt that my tears were joined to the pink river born of those
sheets, and I thought of the priest who had taught me to read
and who had been the first to make use of my body, and I recalled the pain. . . . Everything at once, while I was still empty-
ing myself inside Isabelle, and yet at the same moment too I
was thinking that my aversion to women did not include *her,*
yes, I thought of *her* again . . . thinking that *her* body could never
discharge this evil-smelling red tide, thinking that no one was
using *her* now, thinking how many men had used *her* in the past,
thinking that *she* and I together would do the ceremony of the
flesh in some other way, and I began that very moment to con-
struct the erotic cult for *her,* a new secret ritual that I would be
able to share only with *her,* and which, as it turned out, fell apart
again without my noticing.

I found how to administer *l'herbe folle* as needed, because their life together as well as the moon inclined the women
of The House to menstruate on the same days; and after making mistakes the first few times, I discovered what to give them
to prevent their colic and painful hemorrhages as well as their
inflammations, although I never was a house regular, as le Nègre
Miel had been in his day, because I was not a surgeon while on
land but only practiced my trade while on the freebooters'
expeditions, although, like le Nègre Miel, I did leave a portion
of my scarce seed there in The House, when not inside a man
(to tell the truth, it only took a few times for me to empty

myself), and I learned to bring on (Isabelle also remembered the name of that remedy) the Red Flag in those who were afraid of becoming pregnant and thought they were overdue; and after I took charge until, like a new Sodom, Port Royal was swept from the face of the earth by a gigantic wave—so eager to eradicate the perpetual carousal and other vices from the coast of a clean, radiant, translucent sea—there was not a single offspring conceived in The House.

FOUR

*I*t may be that at one time curiosity had burned brightly
in Pineau; what I was seeing now was that Pineau did not
have the urgency that the ardor of a live curiosity pro-
vokes, for it was in all calmness that Pineau slowly and gradually extracted information from me: yet most of the time asking
much more than I was able to answer him concerning le Nègre
Miel's arts, and often not wanting to know anything about what
I was familiar with. The book he claimed to have found in me
had only a few pages fully written out, in most cases they being
unfinished or smudged. What I felt is that I was rather more
like the shadow of what le Nègre Miel had known in his day,
with many of its features unreadable in me, but perhaps what
Pineau wanted to make me feel was that le Nègre Miel's wisdom, being in itself truncated or incomplete, was often illeg-
ible to *his* eyes. But what is quite certain is that for each bit of
knowledge Pineau obtained from me, he paid me back with
hundreds. He put into my hands the treatise *Briefve collection de
l'administration anatomique* by Ambroise Paré, and when he prac-

ticed his trade in front of me, I had to bring him the dressings I had prepared with the very hands that were holding Paré's book, bring him the scissors, the knives I had sharpened, the chisels and scalpels, and then I cleaned the blood from the table where he had operated. He explained to me that Paré had abolished the custom of treating gunshot wounds with boiling oil; and that he had been the first to practice the substitution of white-hot iron for closing off arteries during an amputation, yet he would never grant me to apply any of le Nègre Miel's remedies on his operating table, not even the ones I knew for decreasing the blood flow from a wound, making pain disappear, making someone sleep, reducing anger, making the heart beat faster . . . Why did he not permit me to do so? What reason, I wondered, did he have for wanting le Nègre Miel's knowledge, if not to use it? I asked him and he did not answer me, he who talked so much and seemed so anxious to teach me, as if wanting the heir to le Nègre Miel's knowledge to forget all of it, overwhelming my faculties in learning the rudiments of being a surgeon's assistant and following his procedures, taking care of the kitchen, of the small vegetable plot we had behind the cabin, cleaning the blood spots from his clothing (*I am a surgeon, not a buccaneer!*), and what most appealed to me, accompanying him on his excursions around the island, for which he always had time except just after the return of some expedition; that was when the badly wounded or poorly cared-for came back from their battles, after having been so inadequately treated by the impromptu barbers they took on board with them. To my great displeasure, I saw for the first time the surgeon opening the skin and laying back the muscles, raking around among the organs looking for a lost bullet. More easily would any pirate become accustomed to the blood, he being impelled by the excitement of the struggle, fighting to save his own skin, than I, peppered by Pineau's words, which would seem to harden when he would strike up against a bone or be struggling against a muscle that resisted him (*Surgery makes a man master of himself;* or, *A surgeon should defend the freedom of man or his freedom of religion and thought*)! To my astonished ears his warm, beautiful words would become firmer when bathed in the whining of the sick man or the spurting of blood or the leg that was finally removed and laid alongside the evil-smelling torso of the patient who seemed to be coming undone in the blood jetting from him! *Surgery is the art that a man practices on his brothers' bodies in order to make the evil more bearable; surgery makes whoever practices it humble* (squish, squash, squish, I would hear the knife going into the muscle—squish—and now it no longer resisted him) *because in it the man joins* (Pineau was putting his hand then into the broken flesh) *the impossible battle against death, and that is a battle that ennobles* (he would remove his hand from within, tugging) *because the enemy always conquers, sooner or later, but always; our lives are made out of the deaths of others, an insensible life remains within the dead material and, joined together again in the stomachs of living beings, it resumes sensual and intellectual life; medicine is the reconciliation of discordant elements; illness is the discordance of elements infused into the living body; our faculties are four in number: memory and intellect, appetite and concupiscence. The first two belong to our rational mind, the others to the senses. The greatest good is wis-*

dom, the greatest evil is physical suffering. The noblest part of the soul is wisdom, the most shameful part of the body is pain. While he was practicing as a surgeon, his intelligence sharpened and he thought with great clarity: mounting to heights that I did not comprehend. Did he not speak of the soul and its highest ideals while struggling amid the darkness the flesh encloses, while dirtying himself in the swamp of the body's filth? The distractions that voraciously surround our intelligence when it wishes to make an appearance were here filtered out by the abject aroma of flesh open to the knife, so that Pineau's intelligence appeared then as splendid, with nothing attempting to check it, absolutely free while his hands were tugging at tendons, trying to control arteries, holding up a palpitating kidney shattered by a clap of gunpowder . . . His words were hard, like walls, like a staircase, hard because they were so true!

On the other hand, when we were watching the astonishing evening light of Tortuga, Pineau's words fell to the ground without a glimmer of illumination, as if they hardly sketched anything out, merely pointed in that direction, making clumsy strokes with efforts that were hesitant, naïve.

"France never had a sky like this."

I, what could I say? I had no words to answer him. I decided to act the mimic. "No, Pineau, never."

"France never had an ocean like this."

"No, never."

"Here the earth seems just recently created."

"Yes, just made."

"It seems to have been created later on."

"Yes, here the earth was created afterward."

"But, how do you dare say that, Smeeks? On the seventh day God rested, and the Holy Scriptures do not say he went back to work making earths again . . . Where did you get that from?"

"I was repeating what you just said, Pineau."

"What are you talking about? Why would I say a thing like that? . . . Look at that strange bird there . . ."

It was just like all the herons that are so numerous along the coast of Tortuga, with a fish dangling from its long beak, Pineau wanting only to distract me with his remark so as to begin again with his "France never had . . ."

Perhaps the fascination he felt for those lands was what moved him to go for long walks from one side of the island to the other, from one to another of the accessible parts of Tortuga. These were not explorations, as Pineau would be covering the same ground he had walked many times over, but he would yet find something new in the forms of the animals, the plants, the texture of the earth, the insects that he trapped in order to observe them, not without arousing my fear and repulsion. He trapped butterflies, spiders (some as big as the palm of my hand), flies of all kinds . . . Afterward he would observe them for hours on end as if they would unlock for him the mysteries of the celestial vault, as if they would sing out the music of the spheres, as if they spoke with words that Smeeks did not hear, up until that moment having been deaf to the forms of life in those lands.

Through le Nègre Miel and Pineau I got an erroneous idea of the island's inhabitants. The cruel nature of my previous master seemed rather the exception. I still did not know that on Tortuga there was no rule, that each man seemed made from a unique mold, but that cruelty was the natural thing in a world floated in blood, because I soon discovered that it was blood and not water that kept Tortuga afloat in the middle of the sea.

fIVE

I did not need that dagger to liberate me from Pineau's service. Weeks before, he had offered me my freedom in exchange for a hundred pesos, due whenever I was able to pay him, without insisting on a fixed date; and I was just waiting for the moment to enlist in the upcoming expedition for which they had already let him know they would be counting on one of his students as the ships' surgeon, with L'Olonnais's blessing. But Pineau was furiously opposed, asking me to wait until some other time, because in spite of being a staunch member of the Brethren of the Coast (and even more, as I would come to realize later on), he did not want to see my heart stained with the blood that was bound to flow profusely on any expedition under Nau's command—L'Olonnais, whom I have already mentioned at the beginning of this book, and who Pineau thought had been left sick and ailing by the blows on the head given him by his buccaneer master, because such a thirst for blood can be nothing but a strange disease; for Nau's illness was assuaged momentarily with blood, only to require it even

more fiercely a few seconds later. Pineau did not have a slave
of his own, black or *matate* or white, and to help him in his work
as a surgeon and fix his daily meals he usually depended on some
young sailor, so that for him to offer me my freedom was all
the more reason to increase my gratefulness to him, he having
made me his right arm; and if he released me in so generous a
way, it was because inside him there lived a good soul.

What I could not get into my head, therefore, when I
saw his body stretched out on the floor of the cabin, was that
anyone might have wanted his death. Was there anyone capable
of wishing evil upon a man like him, who never attempted to
impose anything on anyone, who coveted nothing that belonged
to anyone else, whose only wealth was his yearning for freedom of religion and thought? Although I should have wondered
about this before seeing him motionless there with the dagger
buried in his flesh and finding myself on my knees, attempting
to heal, to sew up, to suture his wound, trying to contain the
uncontainable hemorrhage, crying out to the gods of le Nègre
Miel and begging the All-Powerful not to allow the great Pineau
to die. I should have wondered what a man like him was doing
in the Antilles, a territory where the strong man wins, the deceitful man strives to deceive, the clever man outwits the others; but not where nobility and intelligence have world enough
and time to allow their indelible drop to fall: like a drop of oil,
visible and calming, transparent and useless. I should have asked
myself about all this and not responded lightly, because in that
case I would have reminded myself, "He left Europe in search
of a life where there is freedom of thought. He is living on

Tortuga so that no one will hinder his being a Huguenot, the only law here being force." Without the slightest doubt he had chosen Tortuga because the man who had built the island's fort, who had made the island an impregnable center for contraband and a perfect asylum for pirates, the engineer who had conceived the system of order on the island, had landed there after having been cornered on Saint-Domingue and expelled from La Grande Terre because he was a Huguenot. Pineau talked to me often about Le Vasseur, not only about how, and how ingeniously, he had raised the fortress on Tortuga, turning the island into a key point in the commercial life of the Antilles, and in the trade between the West Indies and Europe. Pineau also recounted hundreds of anecdotes: most of them portraying Le Vasseur as a good man, others as a harsh tyrant. From among the first group I remember the story of the silver Virgin, abducted by some pirates from a Spanish ship, the most valuable article in the whole cargo. The Lieutenant Governor of Saint-Domingue, De Poincy, who had forced the Huguenot Le Vasseur to go to Tortuga, sent him a message requesting the image of the Virgin. Le Vasseur responded by sending a replica carved in wood, with this message as an inscription: *I hasten to obey your order. I remembered that Catholics, because they are so spiritual, love not the material, while we Huguenots, as you well know, prefer the metal, and that is the reason we have had this wood replica made for Your Mercy and why we are keeping the elegant silver image.*

Le Vasseur had certainly reigned in Tortuga more like a king than like a governor. During the twelve years of his rule, he persecuted the residents' slightest infractions with inflex-

ible rigor. He invented a terrifying machine for torture, The
Inferno, through which he made everyone pass who had to
spend time in Purgatory, Tortuga's fortress prison. Whoever
went through The Inferno remained marked forever.

This Calvinist tyrant made an armed citadel out of the
island, choosing the best and most advantageous spot to locate
his fortress, a little distance from the sea, a high rocky platform,
around which he built a series of regular terraces, capable of
quartering up to four hundred men. In the middle of this platform, the rock stood erect thirty feet high in a monticule that
was sheer on all sides, a rather common formation on the island. He built steps only halfway up, and to climb any farther
he used a stairway of iron that he drew up at his convenience,
so that his living quarters and the stores of powder were iso-
lated whenever he wished. At the base of the column of rocks
gushed forth a jet of water as thick as a man's arm, which never
ceased its abundant flow. It was not merely with the fortifications that he took pains. He also looked after the industry (sugar,
the distillery), agriculture, and efficient administration and rule
of his territory, prudently and calmly waiting on Tortuga for
whatever the pirates brought in to do his business and never
making raids on La Grande Terre, as De Fontey, his successor,
would do, inspiring fierce attacks by the Spanish.

Le Vasseur died in an assassination by his two godsons
and protégés whom he had declared successors to his fortune
because of the affection he professed for them: Thiébaut, who
maintained a beautiful prostitute (a constant motive for feud-
ing with Le Vasseur), and Martin. One morning, when Le

Vasseur went down to his warehouse, his two protégés waited
to attack him along with eight others, first with musket blasts
that missed their mark because they confused him with his
image in a mirror he had had brought directly from Murano
(which was made of glass and extremely faithful) in a caprice
that no one understood in him, but which nonetheless saved
him from death for a moment. When he heard the shots, Le
Vasseur, in order to protect himself, ran toward the black who
was carrying his sword, moving out of the mirror's range and
making a real target of himself, upon which Thiébaut inter-
cepted him and killed him by stabbing him with his knife. Before dying, Le Vasseur recognized his beloved murderer and in
his shock, repeated Caesar's remark to Brutus, "Is it you who
kill me, Thiébaut?" and Thiébaut, as if such a remark had dis-
armed him, settled the government on De Fontey (an enemy
of his protector and victim Le Vasseur), abandoned the prostitute, leaving her whatever was now his through his inheritance
from Le Vasseur, and spent the rest of his short life in a hell
comparable to The Inferno, until he put a rope around his own
neck to end his days.

Pineau on the floor did not have the appearance of
wanting to say a last word. That night we had not been alone.
A surgeon's apprentice, come there to relieve me in my duties,
was staying with us, and also a pirate whose wounded knee had
become infected, perhaps because of a splinter still lodged deep
inside; the following morning we were to explore it with surgery to find out. He had arrived close before nightfall, borne
on his companion's shoulder, enveloped in the fetid odor of a

wound in bad state, in search of help and afraid of losing the leg for which he would not even receive compensation now, the booty being already distributed.

Pineau and I were in the habit of chatting until the night was very far gone, though we would go to sleep early if we wished to rise early to undertake one of our endless walks.

In the afternoons I would read and study the treatises of Paré while Pineau would go to the meetings of the Brethren, in the mornings I would sometimes assist Pineau with his operations, and now and then he would allow me to put my hand in while he observed and made remarks; or if not we would go exploring the whole day, even several days in a row, where, listening to Pineau, I learned to observe, to love nature, and to understand the appearance and history of Tortuga, which he knew so well and about which he talked so much.

We would always talk in the dark, and some nights he would seize me by the hips and, mimicking le Nègre Miel with Smeeks or Smeeks with Isabelle, would make use of Smeeks. On one or two occasions I took him to Isabelle, when I was there to administer some remedy and did not feel in the mood to ask for payment, with the object of having him collect it instead, but he seemed as little interested in women as I was at that time; or perhaps I only imagine it, because the truth is that we never spoke directly about our sexual activities with them.

About women, yes. He was the most ardent proponent of forbidding them on Tortuga. He believed the Brethren of the Coast would come crashing down in a heap if women came on the island, that rivalries would enter in, that it would be impossible to go on prohibiting private ownership because everyone would want his woman for himself as an untransferable property, and they in their turn would want their own things and their own land because women do not know how to think about any moral good, that they would take it on themselves to spread envy, that they, being anxious for a more complicated daily life, would infest the island with useless slaves, with a shoddy servant class that would only bring more problems, and many other arguments it would make no sense to note down here, they being not to the point; saving the one that if women serve to clean men of their seed, the body of another man can do that just as well, and better, and whoever does not believe this should practice it, as it does no harm. Moreover, there would never be a shortage of youths on Tortuga, Europe being sure to birth and supply them, and the island relieved of caring for the children.

We were not alone that night, and we were not silent. Something made us laugh, I do not recall what it was, for that night's high spirits have been erased from my memory, as if there were no longer room therein for all our laughter and good feelings, which surely must have irritated the foul-smelling pirate (although behind Pineau's back I had already fixed him up with something to put his wound to sleep, and in truth his leg was more than asleep), on the night of the treacherous murder of Pineau.

Suddenly, a troop of men burst into the dark room without offering a word. It was not just two or three, I calculate there must have been twelve, fifteen, as many as could fit in there, all milling about, bringing a strangely quiet turmoil with them. They quickly pounced on us without giving us time to take up our weapons to defend ourselves. Without understanding what was taking place, I pulled and tugged and screamed out, "Let loose of me, what are you doing?" and what the devil else I shouted at them in the midst of their silence I do not know. A muffled, brief grunt came from Pineau, and I stopped tugging: I knew, I felt, that they had come to murder him. "They," whoever they were.

"We've poisoned le Nègre Miel, like we promised. And now we've stuck it into you, you pigs. We're cattle, cattle, cattle!" They ran out shouting their "cattle!" as I jumped over to Pineau's bleeding body and begged the gods to bring him back to life, enveloped in tears, examining that body pocked with punctures by the dagger, a heart that beat no longer; and hoping to feel the breath that his motionless body no longer exhaled.

(unnumbered chapter

*H*e was not baptized le Nègre Miel but le Nègre Pierre. Bound to the wheel by a long white band of fabric coiled around the neck, he goes around night and day. This gives the lie to the veracity of the story as I have been telling it. Moreover, he is not robust and heavy, with a solid, well-put-together body; the continual movement has distorted his figure, his shoulders are exaggeratedly broad, his buttocks narrow, his legs grotesquely muscular, and his neck, perhaps because of the effect the long white strap produces, is excessively long and thin, topped off by a small, round head.

He turns the wheel; his gaze is lusterless; the strap gleams strangely white, as if it were extremely clean, but it is not clean nor is it so white: the blackness of his skin emphasizes it.

When he is needed they loosen the white strap, setting free his hands and letting it turn above his body, not to untie him, but to release him from the wheel. He bears no sash across his chest, and he never spoke to me. His power is in his words;

he throws seashells on the ground, interpreting the present and foreseeing futures that always come true.

This truth destroys the veracity of my story, the one I have been telling. But we should not be too fixed on this outward appearance, because both are the same one, except that instead of advancing along its horizontal axis I have suddenly moved upward across it, vertically, and this is what I have found. Believe me. This le Nègre Pierre turning the wheel is also true. When his own people and the French discovered his gifts, they bound him to the wheel to keep him from getting away, and that is where le Nègre Pierre spends his days, tied like a mule so the wild beast that he is cannot escape.

Vertical, and not horizontal, as if Madame in the brothel of The House were not going through her room in the natural way, horizontally, but had found how to go through it in upward fashion. She would see, then, instead of the habitual air of elegance and sumptuousness, nothing but abandon and negligence: above the frame holding up the drapes, dead flies and little moths, dust, dereliction, and gloom are what one sees from up there. . . . If she were to describe the room in this way, the room she is writing about would be something else. . . .

And why should I share with the reader the filth that I must clean up all by myself, that must be thrown out because, although it belongs to the room, it is not part of the room? Because, without your closeness, reader, without the warmth and company of your body, I would not have been able to draw the story upward, in a vertical direction, because when your body moves close to mine, I succumb, I let myself go, and in that mode I remain in order to go through the story in a different direction, vertically. . . . That's the way it is when two bodies draw close to each other. The flesh reveals what neither the eye nor the intelligence is able to see. . . . But despite your eroticism, so strong and vigorous, into which I have allowed myself to fall, as into a woman's lap, moving back and forth as I feel you have asked me to do, I do know that the truthfulness of this tale is on the verge of tumbling over the cliff, I know I am capable of collapsing, coming apart, going head over heels— and with me everything that I have written here, that I swear, reader, is true, just as you are or I am when I hold back this pen with my hand before again setting down in ink this true story which we should not allow to be destroyed, or be turned into its own end. Therefore, I promise myself that throughout this book I will not move through the story in any other fashion and that I will direct myself along the horizontal axis so you will believe me, will trust me, will know that it is true, really true. . . . Because this story is the only thing I have for believing myself real.)

END OF PART ONE, which dealt with Smeeks's voyage to Tortuga, his arrival on the island, and how and with whom he learned the office of physician and surgeon.

part the second

which, it is hoped, is less poky,
more fleet of foot, wherein the author and
main character will attempt to
thrust aside his normal inattentiveness,
bewilderment, and melancholy:

The Surgeon
among the Pirates

one

Roc the Brazilian runs through the streets of Port Royal, completely drunk and armed to the teeth, shooting here and there, occasionally wounding someone, waving his sword around without anyone daring to oppose him, either as a challenge or in self-defense. Why? Has everyone gone crazy? I wonder about this while waiting in The House for Isabelle because I need to speak with her, to find out if I can have a word with her. . . . The whole of Port Royal is celebrating. Roc has returned after taking a ship bound from New Spain to Maracaibo, carrying merchandise and a very considerable number of pieces of eight for the purchase of cacao, all of which are now being frittered away in Jamaica. In a single night some of them spend two and three thousand pesos, on which they would be able to live like lords for years, yet in the morning they wake up without even a decent shirt. While waiting for Isabelle I watch one of them promise a whore five hundred pieces of eight just to see her naked, once. She catches me by the hand and, with him stumbling along behind us, completely drunk and totally unaware that I am one of the party, takes me to her room. Pushing me onto a settee, she climbs on top of the bed and stands there, laughing all the while, as she unfastens her long hair and leisurely removes her clothing: never taking her eyes off mine. But I do withdraw my gaze from hers, fixing it on her lovely body, her breasts, her belly, her buttocks, while, at her client's request, she turns slowly around to let us have a good look at all of her. Something I see there that I believe makes her seem very much like *her,* something strange, too, because this one, with her woman's body, is naked, while *she* was always dressed like a man in her deceptive clothing. The moment I become aware of this odd similarity, I am overtaken by a violent erection which flags not one whit as I watch the drunken pirate possess her, fully dressed, with his stupid, repulsive member jutting out from his pants, heaving back and forth with a sullen rapidity that does not explain why he ends up exhausted on the bed, immediately asleep. He makes noises breathing, almost a snore, a whistling, rhythmic sound. Still naked, the whore comes over to me and removes my clothing, all of it. There on the settee we fondle each other lazily and then I possess her without a trace of distaste, not on my part (for the first time) nor on hers. I imagine that this is *she* and I tell her so and she does not understand what I am talking about, yet, putting herself wholly into it as if I were the whore, she participates with all her body along with me in my dark dream.

I do not realize exactly when I ejaculate because we begin again, and again, seemingly unable to free ourselves from one another. The drunken man snores on. I hear someone calling her—"Adèle!"—and we break off as if suddenly the whole thing mattered to us not at all.

"Isabelle isn't going to have time to see you today, I don't know how many are waiting but quite a few. Go take a walk, and come back and sleep with us. You'll be able to talk with her in the morning."

We seem like two gentlemen friends chatting on the settee as we dress hurriedly, freed of the curse of our bodies.

"Don't say anything to anyone about what he gave me for seeing me naked—please, I ask you. I want to get out of here with that money. I've got some more put away. I'm going to go back to my aunt and my brothers. She had to sell me. I'm going back with a full purse, you'll see. Don't say anything to anyone, please don't; not a word, don't repeat this. He's going to forget all about it, and he'll have to pay Madame as if it were a normal service, plus a change of sheets, because for sure he'll vomit. Be nice to me, won't you?"

I promise to be nice even though she is not *her,* and that is what I tell her. And that she hardly seems at all like a woman, and that I appreciate this in her very much.

Out on the street, Roc can no longer be heard shouting around and firing his gun without rhyme or reason. A freebooter has purchased a pipe of wine and, setting it up on a busy street corner where everyone can see, he knocks a hole in the end of it, forcing all who pass by to drink and threatening that if they do not he will shoot them with his pistol; I am told that sometimes he has bought a keg of beer and done the same thing; and that on other occasions he would plunge his hands into the spirits and splash it all over anyone passing by, no matter how messed up their clothing got, men or women. A barrier ring now forms before the spurting jet of wine and around anyone who drinks. No one is standing in front of me. I hear the laughter and jokes of the barricaders. They push me to drink. I hear pistol shots rending the air. Have they all gone crazy? They dance around me as the wine reaches my mouth and runs down my throat. Faceup under the spouting wine I drink, gazing at the unusually blue sky, irritatingly blue, painfully blue, and I drink, and drink, and drink. I am aware of my whole body, unusually happy, irritatingly happy, painfully happy and complete: as if all those who had been using it up till now (or those I had used) had wrenched something from it that was now restored. My entry into the dark mystery of the flesh, I feel with the wine coursing down my throat, has put a new body in place of the other body that used to be me, and for the first time in days I am not angry, for the first time since Pineau's death, and for the first time in my seventeen years I am for the first time drunk and for the first time whole, on my own two feet, reeling along the streets brimming with music, joining in with the celebration where everything is offered so freely, hearing stories here and there that to my inexperienced nostrils smack more of boastfulness than of the bloody business they claim to be so full of, even though they are closer to the truth than my own nostrils on this lovely night just beginning.

two

I did keep quiet, but my silence was not enough to protect Adèle, just as the fact that she had indulged me with the secrets of her body was not enough for me to feel tied to her in the way I did to my *she*.

What makes a body get *sick* over another body, to absolutely need another? How does the mechanism of magnets work? Not even though she had generously bestowed on me that extravagant arousal and exquisite revelation did I feel *sick* for her. Sometimes it is just the opposite, the *sickness* or suffering arising from the fact that there is no yielding, that no surrender comes of it, that their bodies are not permitted to explode with desire. I will have to cite Morgan after all, even though I promised not to speak of him. After the assault on Panama, he remained ashore, sending out patrols of two hundred men to bring in the loot from the surrounding area. On one of those days, a portion of the prize they found was a woman of exceptional beauty and, according to the claims of her own people, great virtue. Morgan felt attracted by her, *sick* for her, and ordered that she be given special treatment, separating her from the other prisoners; and he devoted himself to seducing her, with fortune both good and bad at once—good because the woman altered the opinion she formerly held concerning pirates and wondered why such men had been described to her as brutes, as savages without feeling, if indeed they were re-fined human beings, educated and thoughtful; and bad because she still refused to give in to Morgan's suggestions. The nor-mal thing for Morgan would have been to take her by force, as he did with so many women on those raids, but, his body being *touched* by that woman, he still persisted; until he understood that it was totally useless, and then he gave orders that her fine clothes be torn off her body and that she be shut up in a filthy prison where she received little food and water, but which was nonetheless comfortable and even luxurious in comparison with the sumptuous bed of that pirate who was burning for her, hungry for *her,* desperately thirsty for *her* body, sick because of *her,* tortured invisibly by his passion for *her.* What did his *she* have that drove him so mad, a man who was accustomed to setting the ransom price on women and also to reaping the immediate carnal harvest he and his men wrested, almost with-out looking at them, from any women who crossed their path? When he abandoned the city—or rather the spot the city had occupied, it being now completely destroyed, the whole place turned into spoils and plunder or else into empty terrain where anything that lay exposed was devastation and ruin: enormous piles of broken things destroyed by the gluttonous high spirits of Morgan and his men (among whom I was one)—he took the woman with him, together with the prisoners for whom he had received no recompense, as well as those his men had rounded up in the wilderness, threatening them with death in two days if their indemnities did not arrive in time.

Messengers went back and forth, but to come forth with the ransom payments for most of them was impossible. Since the surrounding countryside had already been combed over by Morgan's fierce patrols, where would they get the money, with everything sacked and nothing left standing?

The husband of the woman who had made Morgan sick found himself on business outside Panama and, having learned of the siege, had not returned. He was not one of those who had fled in good time with some of their men while leaving women and children behind when they heard the pirates were approaching, as some were accustomed to doing in the Caribbean; he yet remained at a prudent distance, and with his pockets full. He was located in time by a priest in her trust who returned on the day of the execution of the prisoners with the ransom price Morgan demanded in exchange for her; except that here the priest did a better business, because he freed three that he knew would pay him three times the amount—each one—the moment they were reunited with their families. News of this reached her ears, and she confronted Morgan in order to tell him so (*Do you think,* she used the familiar pronoun *tú* with him, *that it is right what this man of God, who had my greatest confidence, has done to me?*), whereupon he ordered the priest to be seized in exchange for her freedom.

Thus the priest was the only one not already half dead of thirst and hunger whose lot it was to suffer such butchery the night Morgan left that land till then unplanted by man now

sown with arrow-pierced bodies. They looked something like
mangled toys, those bodies, 185 men and women, unburied,
whose stench after a few days must have guided those who
arrived too late with the ransom payment, too late with their
futile entreaties for Morgan to release their friends or family
members.

Yes, I did keep quiet about this one body who sold
herself naked and also about her plan to flee, even though she
was no magnet to me and perhaps even because she was not.
But when she left The House, *before,* she thought, *the word gets
around and I'm forced to cough up my purse,* she had to wait for the
departure of the ship that kept putting it off, waiting for the
supplies that should already have arrived from Veracruz: Puebla
biscuits and dried fish. Immediately, creditors real and ficti-
tious fell upon her. There was one who claimed to be the owner
of the bed she had been using and who charged her for it, he
said, *because you have rendered it useless,* she fighting back with the
argument that not only had she not left it useless but she had
spent twice its price in trimming and decorating it, and she was
leaving it so, trimmed and decorated. And there was another
who wanted to collect for the full month's room and board plus
the following two months, because how would they be able to
get someone so quickly, just like that, to make up for her? and
she, not having announced her departure ahead of time so she
could be replaced, was bound to pay this, although it was true
that she could leave now, having already fulfilled her three years
of service some six months back—yet for those six months she
still owed them for the room, the use of the bed, her meals,

the washing of sheets, her cosmetics, the new clothes demanded by the elegant atmosphere of The House but which she would have to leave behind upon her departure because they did not belong to her (she discovered this just now, all of a sudden) and she had only been paying for the wear and tear on them. She argued that she would not pay for her meals as she was not going to be eating them and that if she did have to pay for them she would not pay for the bed, to which they responded that the payment for the bed had nothing to do with the payment for the meals because the bed belonged to someone else, the two things having nothing to do with each other. And one night some rogue broke into the room she was renting until the ship left, which should be any day now, it was even said that the supplies from Veracruz had already arrived; and when she cried out for help, more young men arrived, but only to rob her: whoever did not carry off her dress, which she had taken off for sleeping, stole her wig or her hat, and whoever did not make off with her hose or her shoes . . . In a few days she had no other recourse than to return to work, because with what she had left there was scarcely enough to pay for her passage on the ship, which was carrying slaves and people of the worst sort, and not enough to pay for her food; and to arrive there with empty hands would be a guarantee that she would be sold once more by her poor aunt, and again she would have to leave that poor aunt and go away, who knows where, far away from her beloved brothers, to start all over from scratch. . . .

THREE

After the murder of Pineau, my first impulse was to get away from Tortuga. Although through him I had learned to love it, the place now repulsed me as the land that was sheltering his murderers. There was not time enough to bring this first impulse to pass. A second one erupted immediately, and more forcefully: not to abandon Tortuga until I found out whose hand it was that held the knife which killed Pineau, the hand that poisoned le Nègre Miel slowly with that substance I was not familiar with and which brought on his melancholy, his loss of interest in living, his desire to give in, and finally his death: a poison on which, if I were to baptize it, I would lay the name of "desolation." I began by suspecting that Pineau's purchase of me may well have been, yes, because I was the book written by le Nègre Miel, but especially because of one page that had tempted Pineau's heart so much that he contradicted his principles with regard to slavery; yet now I did not think le Nègre Miel's wisdom was the reason for it, since Pineau had roundly refused to make use of his arts and would look on with reprehension in his eyes whenever I picked up some herb—but because of a page that Smeeks himself was unaware of. Could it be that le Nègre Miel had not written it? If that were the case, it might well be connected somehow with The House in Port Royal, since he had also kept silent about all that. Then I was assaulted by wild fantasies which featured menstrual blood in some strange way, but I frightened them off, knowing they were absurd, and I became aware of not being able to think clearly, of being unable to tie up the loose ends, of being totally at a loss, of not comprehending, once again, that Smeeks understood nothing at all about any of this. Who had killed them? For what reason had they been killed?

Passing in review the people they both would visit frequently, searching for coincidences, yet was I unable to come up with anything other than the afternoons when le Nègre Miel and Pineau absented themselves from me in order to attend the Society's meetings, wherever it was they met. Certain that the answer would lie there, on those afternoons when I was not with them, those afternoons which were forbidden me, I had gone to Jamaica to have a word with Isabelle.

I never did get to talk to her. I stayed drunk for several days and do not recall whether I went to The House even once to sleep it off or whether I slept at all or ate or anything else that happened to me, because I lost all consciousness of myself; and when I regained it I was signing a paper with a name that was not mine, had never been mine, and on which I had let fall a drop of my blood. My signature said, "Le Trépaneur."

The paper was the Contract prepared by the Admiral before our departure:

Laus Deo.

We owe obedience only to God, apart from whom there is no other master in these lands but ourselves, lands over which, risking our lives, we have wrested dominion from a country which in its turn has usurped them from the Indians.

These are the rules of the contract that every freebooter must follow:

Article 1. We, the signers below, receive and recognize L'Olonnais as our good Admiral, with the following conditions:

that if any of us disobeys him in anything he may command, he is allowed to punish such a man in acccordance with his crime; or that he will desist from doing so, if the majority of votes goes against him.

Article 2. As Vice Admiral we recognize Antoine Du Puis, and as Captain on Land, Michel Le Basque.

Et cetera, et cetera. The Contract set out the basis for the division of the booty, down to the last detail, as well as the compensation for the loss of one eye or both, of one or both legs, of fingers, hands, and arms, under the supposition that if there is no booty there is no payment; but that whoever lost any part of his body would be owed his share until enough booty became available, if not on the expedition that we were under-taking, then on the following one, or on as many expeditions as might be necessary to pile up the amount with which the rest of the pirates would be able to settle the debt they were promising in advance to be responsible for.

After the signing of the Contract, we all embarked for Tortuga. I picked up my things, the surgeon's tools that had been Pineau's up till then, and some weapons that had also belonged to him. I would not be telling the truth were I to say that an enormous sadness overwhelmed me when I went into the cabin to get them, I would not be telling the truth because that was not what I felt. A grim fit of distractedness struck me. I was nowhere around, although I was there. Suddenly I found myself kicking poor Euripedes, a dog we used to take care of in exchange for his looking after us, which he did very well because he always defended the doorway to the cabin—*except on the night they murdered Pineau.* I delivered several blows just because I ran into him, as if my stupidness were his fault, with-out even recalling his silence the night of Pineau's death. He dropped his head and allowed my arrogant spirit to descend upon him. He did not even growl or show his teeth. Suddenly I was ashamed, the blows bringing me back to the cabin I had shared with my beloved Pineau, and the memory of him show-ered down on me, shook me up, left me in pieces, scarcely able to stand. I stooped over to scratch the dog behind the ears, yet Euripedes did not return my gaze. It was all over between us.

I never went back to the cabin. Whenever I returned to Tortuga, I would sleep any old where, like the other pirates, nor did I practice as a surgeon while on land as Pineau had done. That day I loaded up my things and slept in the forest on Tortuga to get more herbs for my remedies, crowding as much as possible into the last little corner of time before the moment of departure.

Everything being well prepared, with 1,670 men in eight ships, after making an inspection of the arms we each one of us would rely on and the artillery aboard the ships, we set sail at the end of April and proceeded toward Bayala on the northern coast of Hispaniola to take on enough smoked meat for the voyage. There, a party of hunters joined us of their own free will, having provided us with all manner of necessary supplies. We spent May and June on that part of the island. There, in actuality, my life as a pirate began. I attached myself to them, sleeping a dream called "surprise," and when we arrived at Bayala I began to live like they did, sleeping every night in a different place. I realized that ever since leaving Europe I had been living like a woman, repeating the routine of going to sleep every day in the same protected corner and at about the same hour. There are so many who live that way—like women, shut up behind the walls of a convent, a prison, a house, a shop, hidden behind the many skirts of the one single place that shields them with its constant *being there*! . . . From that day on, and for many years (thirty-seven), I lived a constant challenge to the sun, the wind, following the inclemencies of the strange, luminous nature of the Caribbean. . . . We freebooters are the mirror of the day, of the untamed ocean waves: the mirror of the squall, the storm, the fiercely cruel wind called

Huracán! To be able to be this reflection of the days as they go by, we reject any routine, every routine. We do not eat every day, but when we do eat, our tables are always set differently: sumptuous and costly, or simply meager, but never the same: tables set for those who do not live like women!

I stopped being Smeeks and became one of the Brethren in the Society of the Coast, and was baptized by them under the name of Le Trépaneur (a word which means someone who bores into the skull), as I said before, and as I told myself day and night in order to convince myself of it, to understand it, to know it, to make it so.

I had not found out who murdered Pineau and poisoned le Nègre Miel. I had no past, though in my present life the pair of them gave me support as a full member of the Society, and if it were not for them I would be an apprentice on trial, a matelot like all the other recent arrivals when they joined the Society. Pineau and le Nègre Miel, with the trade they had taught me together, had provided my initiation as a pirate. Moreover, everyone knew that Le Trépaneur was the heir to le Nègre Miel's wisdom and the one that Pineau had trained, and consequently it was I who stood for the things they had defended with their deaths, although I did not realize it then. Just as I never realized anything, scatterbrained as I used to be, and still am, because of the way I am made up, for my mind fixes its attention rather on vain, superfluous things than on what is definitive or principal. I repeated a phrase to myself: *This is the hour of Le Trépaneur!* and in that phrase, without my knowing it, I was upholding, in the way that le Nègre Miel and Pineau had taught me to do, the survival of the wisest law ever made for mankind, the Law of the Coast, the root, trunk, and fruit of the Society of the Brethren that on Tortuga makes men into the most generous beings, as well as the fiercest, ready to wrest from the Spaniards what no one can ever defend as belonging to them.

I, who used to be a pirate and defended the Society at risk of my life and who now am nothing but a scribbler, jotting things down on a sheet of paper in order that the memory of le Nègre Miel may not fade, I still become emotional after hundreds of years (in my memory) over the dream of the Brethren of the Coast.

four

❧

E n route to Punta de Espada our good fortune began, when we sighted a ship coming from Puerto Rico loaded with cacao for New Spain. But this first battle would also be one for our eyes only: we had to wait for L'Olonnais on La Isla Saona, south of Punta de Espada, so that he could take on the prize all alone.

The battle lasted three hours, after which they surrendered to L'Olonnais. The prize was mounted with sixteen guns, and it carried fifty men to defend it, as well as 120,000 pounds of cacao, forty thousand pieces of eight, and jewels to the value of ten thousand pesos. It was sent to Tortuga to be unloaded and with orders to return immediately because L'Olonnais wanted it for himself in order to give the one he had to Antonio Du Puis. While it was on the way back to us we took another ship, one that had come from Comaná with arms, powder, and shot, in addition to the payroll for the soldiers on the island of Santo Domingo.

Little idea did I have from these encounters of what an attack by pirates was like, because L'Olonnais happened to be in too nice a mood and simply pardoned the defeated ones— though by this I mean that he just threw them overboard in order to avoid having to put any food into Spanish maws, thus killing them quickly and without demonstrating his natural cruelty; and so often having been told about the clever way he had escaped from Campeche after witnessing the festivities mounted to celebrate his own death (as I will relate here), to- gether with many other entertaining episodes concerning him, I had gotten a mistaken notion of the freebooters' thirst for blood, one that tinged it with lightness, with humor and charm.

L'Olonnais's ship foundering in a storm near the coast of Campeche, the crew reached the shore where the ruthless Spaniards, apprised of the shipwreck, were already waiting for them with drawn swords and loaded muskets in order to anni- hilate them altogether, congratulating themselves on their good luck and expecting to be easily able once and for all to finish off the savage L'Olonnais.

Soon wounded, and not knowing how else he might save his life, he gathered up some handfuls of sand, mixed it with blood from his wounds, spread this on his face and other parts of his body, and stealthily arranged himself among the dead, waiting until the Spaniards left the spot.

Then he stole the clothing off a dead Spaniard and car- ried it with him into the jungle nearby, where he hid himself and bandaged his wounds as best he could so they would not become infested with mosquitos and worms; then he disguised himself as a Spanish gentleman and threaded his way toward Campeche.

The city was burning candles to celebrate his death. He struck up a friendship with a slave, and, after giving him a chance to tell all about his troubles and, in the process, reassuring himself of the fellow's hatred for his master, L'Olonnais promised him freedom, immunity, and membership in the Brethren of the Coast if he obeyed him and trusted him. The slave undertook to enlist others in the same plight, and at night they stole a canoe from one of their masters and set out on the open sea with the pirate, where they paddled constantly, thrilled to be so near their freedom, until they reached Tortuga. What a pretty picture, that of the pirate escaping even as the city was giving thanks for his death!

I heard this and other tales while we were taking on supplies before our departure, or else waiting for the capture of the ships and their return from Tortuga, stories like the one about the aristocrat Jean François de la Roque, Seigneur de Roberval, wrongly called Roberto Baal by the Spaniards (who mix everything up in their slapdash language), and second in command to Jacques Cartier, the discoverer of Canada and Lieutenant Governor of all the lands discovered by order of Francis I, King of France; who, choosing piracy over glory, attacked Santiago de Cuba in 1543. Or the one about the uncle of Montbars, "The Exterminator," who, when he saw his small vessel cut off and about to be taken, had it blown up rather than surrender it to the odious Spaniards. Or the one about Montbars himself: The night before their departure on an ambitious expedition, Montbars invited all his captains to a council in order to decide which place they would assault, considering the forces available and how long their resources would last. While the captains were enjoying themselves in the quarterdeck cabin, everyone else was doing the same on deck, and all of them, even the surgeons, were drunker than the wine. By accident, a spark fell into the store of gunpowder, and the ship blew sky high with everyone on board. As on this ship the powder was stored in the forecastle, those in the cabin at the stern suffered little harm except to find themselves in the water, but three hundred of their men were drowned. The expedition was delayed by this event, yet after a week fifteen vessels and 970 freebooters weighed anchor for Maracaibo (just like ourselves) where they tricked a newly arrived Spanish fleet with a fire ship (a bark filled with straw and gunpowder that was sent against the enemy ships to set them afire) in which they set up a dummy pirate crew with old straw hats on sticks. Before setting it loose, Montbars said to his men, *The arrival of the squadron is splendid news; the Spanish are giving us a glorious victory. Be brave! Those shitheads will see our faces, but we will see only their backs!* (I recall seeing him years later, cruising in the Gulf of Honduras. He was astute, alert, and brimming with energy, like all Gascons, olive-skinned, tall, erect, and quite strong, there being no one able to get the better of him one-on-one. It is hard for me to describe the color of his eyes with certainty because his thick, dark eyebrows closed in an arc above them and covered them almost completely, so much so that his eyes seemed hidden inside a dark cave. Yet everyone knew at first sight that this was a man to be feared, that he conquered through the terror induced by his gaze.)

Or the story about Pierre Le Grand, sailing in a small ship, almost out of supplies but with twenty freebooters aboard ready to take on any Spanish merchantman, when he came up against a frigate with seventy-five cannons and two hundred men. The pirate did not hesitate. He sank his own ship, stormed the Spaniard, and launched himself toward the powder stores with a lighted match, ready to blow the ship into pieces if the crew did not put down their arms. Faced with this energetic charge, the surprised Spaniards surrendered. The officers who tried to continue the fight were slaughtered, and Pierre Le Grand had himself a prize that made him rich for the rest of his life.

This was the colorful and triumphant tone of those stories. I never heard them describe how prisoners are tortured, none mentioning what took place when Montbars found Maracaibo deserted but still got hold of two prisoners, an old man, more than seventy, and a young man accompanying him. A slave claimed the old man was rich, whereupon Montbars put him to the ropes, attaching them by the man's four extremities and stretching his limbs toward the four corners of the room, whereupon he confessed to owning nothing but the hundred crowns the young man carried with him. The pirates did not believe him and went on with the torture, which they call "dry swimming," but now placing a stone that weighed hundreds of pounds on his torso while four men tightened the ropes that held him, and as he yet would not confess to anything further, they built a fire beneath him until it scorched his flesh. They dealt with the youth in like fashion and afterward strung him up by the testicles until they were almost wrenched off him, at length sword-whipping him and casting him into a ditch. A prisoner taken later on said that the youth still lived. No, I heard none of the infinite number of tales repeated that would have allowed me to get an idea of what their cruelty was like. *Our* cruelty, because in a few days, we too would take Maracaibo.

I must describe something about Maracaibo, but not the beauty of the town, its houses and hospitals and convents and markets, because none of this remained standing. Nor will I say anything either about the beauty of their women, because we ruined them as well, maltreating them even as they humbled themselves before our vileness, satisfying all our whims just to get bread out of us, or the flour to make it, or some meat or fruit, but most of the time in order to calm the hunger of their poor children, who would die anyway because the occupation lasted so long that no child could resist the hunger and the thirst, water also being scarce.

Neither will I talk about the dignity of their buildings, nor the cleverness and extent of their industry, nor of how excellently their cattle were kept in the surrounding area and on the neighboring islands, the interior being of little use as pasture land, although on the other hand prodigal with fruit; nor will I spin eulogies over their dense plantations of cacao, nor their roads so well planned and laid out, nor their carts and mules, nor their well-equipped strongholds, nor the fortress rising up on the Isla de las Palomas, with its palisade formed of stakes and earth, equipped with fourteen cannons and 250 men—the first thing we attacked and destroyed.

I will not talk about what was not left standing, about what was not preserved from our fury, but of the loveliness of the bay, that some call the Gulf of Maracaibo, and about the Bravo Indians, natural enemies of the Spanish and thus our allies, and a people whose children did survive our wrath. These Bravos helped us get into the bay, and without them it would have been virtually impossible to take so well defended a region with so little cost in lives.

The Bravos, so designated by the Spanish because of their uncompromising courage and their untamable spirits, lived on the islands and islets in the lake of Maracaibo. To save their skins they had left their natural territory on dry land to their enemies. According to them, the name of the lake used to be Coquibacoa, and they paid no attention to the way we called it; although they informed us that the name Maracaibo had been that of a cacique who ruled the region once, an area only recently taken by the Spanish. In 1529 Ambrosio Alfingui founded a village on the site, but as soon as he died, his successor, Pedro San Martín, perhaps because the heat in that region is never mitigated by the feeble breezes or because running water is very scarce, abandoned the village, the Indians then destroying it. Around 1571 Alonso Pacheco founded a city with fifty men, but had to abandon it after three years of intense struggles with the Bravos, who call themselves *Aliles* or *Bobures* or *Moporos, Quiriquires, Tansares, Toas,* or *Zaparas,* depending on insignificant differences in their customs, using many names for what is all the same to our eyes. In 1574, Pedro Maldonado, with only thirty-five men, managed to wrest the territory from the Indians and founded La Nueva Zomar where Maracaibo is now, the which, when we captured it, had already been twice devastated by pirates; by which it is proven that, given that the Spaniards stole these lands through evil, we had the right to take what they had received from the bounteousness of the lands they had stolen. Because who paid any heed to the Pope, that lackey of the Spanish Crown, whose bull claimed that the Caribbean Sea and the Antilles belonged to Spain? A *papal* bull? What authority could he have over us when his robes are embroidered with gold given him by the Spanish Crown? As for we who practiced piracy, it was not for us to restore order to the way it used to be but instead to appropriate what had no reason to belong to them: the first treasure of importance that Cortés sent to the Spanish king being seized by Giovanni da Verrazano, called Juan Florín by the Spaniards, in the spirit of their language because, as I have already mentioned, say what you like to a Spaniard, he always finds a way to make it over in his own language.

Coquibacoa, our Maracaibo, the Bravos . . . As their only dress, the men wore belts of cotton embroidered with stones, very much like those I had seen on the skeletons of the Grottoes of the Plain, the enormous pit on Tortuga that I went down into with Pineau; and the women wore around their hips a piece of cloth that would be of different lengths depending on their age and rank. The youngest were almost naked, and they never stopped laughing and showing their teeth. As they were our allies, we never touched any of their women, except L'Olonnais, who as a show of friendship was given three women, perfect in every way except for their skin being painted all over with bright colors for the occasion, and their hair being fixed in a strange fashion, as if dampened with mud and then molded into an unnatural, whimsical shape; although to tell the truth, I do not really know if he ever touched them, because in front of us he let be seen the disgust produced by their naked bodies, above all when they were no longer marked with the dye, which happened almost immediately, as the peoples of that land habitually bathed one or more times every single day, something that never ceased to astonish us; and the paint they used on their skin ran with the water, unlike the dyes they used so skillfully for their clothing. Yet even as they disquieted him, he was also moved to laughter (something very unusual in him) to see how we, his men and his boys, stared at them and at the other women, all of them naked. At first I kept quiet, not knowing what to feel, as their nakedness did not look at all like what I had seen on one of the beds in Port Royal; their open nudity in the light of day had something grotesque about it, especially in the shape of their breasts, tipped with such enormous nipples, the way they showed their teeth when they laughed, and their feet, and their black hair, gleaming and loose, most of the time long enough to cover their shoulders and sometimes even their skirts.

Their houses were raised above the trees or on poles jutting up over the surface of the lake, by which they avoided the insidious mosquitos, as well as the flooding when the lake rose—which was quite often, what with the dozens of rivers opening out into the lake (Catatumbo is the most beautiful and the swiftest)—and also cooling down the unbearable heat. They built their piraguas (that is what they called their canoes) out of a single tree trunk, into which they would fit up to eighty crewmen. They used to put poison on the tips of their arrows, really enormous arrows, as long as the men themselves were tall; taking up the shells of various-sized conches, they would break them up and use the pieces (as hard as European glass), after working them over with infinite patience, to give the bows and the arrows their final appearance and firmness.

The men and the women used different languages, one for each group, though for work both alike would use their backs. When at peace, the men had more than enough time to throw themselves into their hammocks. But the women never did: they sowed the seeds, they cared for the yucca plants, they dug out the cassava roots, they replanted the plots, they peeled the roots and grated them and allowed them to expel their poison, they prepared the bread with the flour, they baked it, they hunted small animals for meat, they took care of the children—how could they possibly spend their afternoons in a hammock (which they wove) for the simple pleasure of watching time go by?

It was the Bravos who worked out the strategy for the capture of Maracaibo, making themselves understood to us through an interpreter who spoke beautiful French. They led L'Olonnais and his men into the first reaches of the entrance to the gulf or sea of Maracaibo. They had some men spying here and there, overcoming or enduring the unpleasant swamps that bordered the numberless rivers, and observing the fortifications and their emplacements; through whom we were opportunely able to become aware of many things for our protection or our defense, as when on the assault of the fort (the first place we attacked when our boats had scarcely even dropped anchor before the entrance to the lake, reaching land quickly in the piraguas the Indians lent us, moving them rapidly, skillfully, and in total silence) we vanquished the Spaniards, surprising them and disabling the rear guard they had placed there to entrap us.

In that first assault we killed every Spaniard we could. The ones they had placed behind us to surprise us managed to escape, but being unable to return to the fort they therefore made their way as fast as they could to the city to announce, "Two thousand pirates are coming, well armed and organized!" All the inhabitants left the city, taking their riches with them, their women, their children, their slaves. When we arrived at Maracaibo with our ships and set up a hot fusillade from our position on the water against their fortifications and their forests, we had no reply, everyone having already left. The houses were empty, the streets empty, even the slaves were frightened away by us. In the whole city there beat only one heart: a newborn baby was crying in a crib, abandoned, perhaps, so something of more use or greater value could be carried in someone's hands.

We disembarked in the city and made ourselves comfortable in the best buildings, storing our weapons and battle supplies in the church. L'Olonnais set up a watch to protect us while we celebrated the not-so-glorious capture of Maracaibo; up till now we had needed to attack only the fort that guarded the entrance to the lake, and that we subdued through the cleverness and the spies of the Bravo Indians, our allies.

All the same, as if our victory had been worthy of it, during those first days we celebrated. Maracaibo had enough and to spare for the dressing of our tables and the warming of our throats, and so we wined and dined sumptuously.

Except for one pirate, Mum (so baptized because not even when asleep did he ever stop talking), who cooed day and night at the newborn child we discovered, giving him cow's milk to drink, singing to him and washing diapers and sheets, crazy with happiness over this portion of the loot, which he was nonetheless to abandon in his turn when we started the march on Gibraltar.

five

Rafael Marques was wearing a long, velvety cloak, disguised (he said) as Queen Metecona of Blue Island, blue being the color of the long cloak Marques had devised to wear over his own clothing, having appropriated the drapes of one of the splendid houses we had taken. Rafael Marques was not yet a freebooter, he was a matelot being tried out by the Society: one whose bravery was in the balance and upon whom every eye was scrupulously fixed, watching him more carefully than anyone else who wished to enter the Brethren of the Coast, for he was Spanish, to judge from his name, though he called himself Portuguese, and moreover it was said that his life had been spared when the ship he had been serving on was taken by pirates; and there was even more: that instead of having been put off in the first port or marooned on the first little island they touched at, he had been allowed provisional acceptance if he was able to pass the trials as a matelot before entering the Society. Because he it was who had shown Pierre Le Grand where the ship he had just attacked kept its powder stores and enabled him to make that threat, with match lit, of blowing up the ship if they didn't surrender; and he it was who had then removed his companions' weapons out of their reach. Afterward he explained to Pierre Le Grand that he had been eagerly hoping for the arrival of some freebooter craft, as he found life with the Spaniards not to his liking and wished to join up with the Brothers. Whether Pierre Le Grand believed him or not, whether his story was true or not, no one knew for a certainty, because after that celebrated assault, Pierre Le Grand had returned to the continent with such riches as enabled him to spend the rest of his life there, never going back to sea. Neither were we able to know if the other things Rafael Marques told about himself were true, for example, that in Portugal he had written and published poetry, that he had left the mainland as secretary to an ambassador, that the Spaniards had brought him into discredit; and as these stories that carried him successively to the ship attacked by Pierre Le Grand and thence to L'Olonnais yet seemed rather odious to us because of something that would disappear once his trials were successfully passed, that is, his Spanish name, we were somehow patient with him and the unpleasant impression he made on us, trusting that when he was accepted into the Society and lost his Spanish name we would be able to see him more sympathetically; which was an assumption that proved false, like the rest of his story, per- haps—because we would need to accept him before allowing him to enter the Society.

Queen Metecona of Blue Island, though in possession of another name, went on being Rafael Marques beneath the long cloak: making jokes at our expense in that uncontrollable and well-founded intoxication we had acquired at the abundant tables of Maracaibo. She strolled all around the streets we had marked as our territory, inspecting everything (we were unaware of that) and getting as far as the guard posts in order to observe their movements.

Queen Metecona of Blue Island kept talking and talking as she minced and curtsied before us, joking about how much Her Majesty owed to Our Highnesses.

Suddenly, Queen Metecona of Blue Island disappeared. No one noticed her absence immediately because for those of us who had quaffed and eaten our fill it was time to sleep now, while for those who were merely stuffed to the gills it was time to go on watch, and for those already on watch it was time to sit down to drink and gorge themselves until dawn.

Rafael Marques moved far enough away in the darkness to be able to go on without danger in the full morning sunlight, by then out of our sight. During the time we had been drinking and eating—which we were in sore need of doing, having had very scant nourishment during the respite before the assault—he was thinking, calculating, making plans, and convincing himself that, we being so many but also so drunk and now also without our allies the Bravos, with whom we had agreed to share the booty when it was collected together, he would be able to gain more from our assault if he jumped ship and revealed to the Spaniards what to do to defeat us, since, we being so intoxicated and also unaccompanied by the Indians, with him or without him we were going to be defeated; and he, fearing to find himself amongst the vanquished, took flight under cover of his identity as Queen Metecona of Blue Island—not realizing that it was the swamps on the Maracaibo side that had loosed the humors impairing his good sense, if it is true that Rafael Marques had ever had any.

SIX

When I began to relate my story, it was established that I would have the eyes and ears of Smeeks, Le Trépaneur, or Exquemeling, whichever name I or the others would use to designate me. In the order of the story, first I was Smeeks, then came the ceremony (which I ought to describe in more detail, relating, for example, how the one who is becoming a Brother drinks the blood of the other Brothers and in turn lets his own blood so that they may drink of it, all mixed with wine; but, in order the more quickly to reach the end of my story, I did not wish to pause over every least detail); but I believe that from the beginning I have been Exquemeling, because he it is who, though of no importance in himself, usually narrates my story, so as not to call attention to the person of Smeeks.

The moment has come when eyes and ears do not suffice to continue. I now have need of Smeeks's heart, Le Trépaneur's heart, Exquemeling's heart. Because what would these eyes see in that attack by the cruel L'Olonnais on the ship that came after the heads of his crew, a ship sent out by the governor in Havana, fully equipped and with orders to hunt L'Olonnais down and kill all his men, supplied also with an executioner to carry out the beheadings, commissioned as such by the governor himself? They would see so much blood as would cloud over the narration and they would lose their way, like the Spaniards before us when, after the above-mentioned attack on Maracaibo, we went after the neighboring town of Gibraltar and they resisted us with so extravagant an expense of gunpowder as to make them blind amid the billows of smoke given off by the gunfire, losing sight of us, strangely enough, and losing control totally; while we ourselves kept from losing our heads—there was good reason not to, one had to be cold-blooded, this was not a party or a drunken binge but war—and we were able to take them by surprise. These eyes would see so much blood: that of the whole crew including the black executioner, who weeping implored them not to kill him, claiming that he was the captain of that ship and would give L'Olonnais as much information as he wanted; to which L'Olonnais agreed, hearing him out until the man had nothing more to give him, and then, without softening, made his blood to run. Only one man remained alive (and he did not even ask for pity) to serve as L'Olonnais's messenger to the governor, though he was nearly incapable of carrying out his charge because the sight of so many bloody deaths had unhinged him, and in his disordered mind the only words there seemed room for were those of the black executioner, the strong and until then imperturbable man who from his great height had bawled out, "Have pity!" something that he himself had never shown toward those he had put to death, and who knows how many of them there were; by reason of which the poor man could not manage to say, *I am the messenger to the governor,* after our men had left him in a canoe on the wharf at Havana, but instead he shrieked: *Have pity on me, don't kill me, I am the captain, I will answer whatever you ask, have pity . . . ,* trembling grotesquely all the while, exactly as the huge black executioner had done, he of the firm, steady hand. Nor would he have handed over the letter had it not been that someone recognized him and told them who he was (or who he used to be before going mad), and this same person, in describing the character of the madman, explained that the now insane man had been aboard the ship sent in pursuit of L'Olonnais, as all the while the messenger, repeating the same phrase with such persistent vigor that no one understood why he did not calm down, why his voice remained so clamorous, was holding out his arms whose hands clasped between them the pirate's letter that said, *I will never give quarter to the Spaniard. I have the firm expectation of doing the same thing to your person as was done to all those aboard your ship, by which you sought to do the same to me and my companions.* They carried the messenger into the presence of the governor so he could receive L'Olonnais's letter into his own hands; whereupon the governor, taken by a fear so uncontrollable that he was unable to hold back, shot the unfortunate man: the one who once upon a time had embarked on the mission ordered by the governor, then became a survivor, then lost his mind, then shrieked tirelessly like the executioner, and suddenly was finished off; which put the governor into a double predicament: that of knowing himself threatened by the cruel, much-feared L'Olonnais, and that of being the murderer of an innocent man. So that, in order to escape one of the two situations, the trigger had scarcely been pressed when the governor began to call out for them to find the man responsible for the murder he himself had mistakenly committed, pretending he had not done it: an act that was welcomed by his followers there because it looked bad to them that the governor, being so frightened, had done what no one would ever admit he had done, in an attack of panic, under the stupid belief that the vicious pirate's threat would disappear with the death of the unfortunate messenger.

So they cast around for the one who had shot the messenger and they found a young man who had been passing by the spot, and even though he was not carrying a firearm they were pleased to think him guilty. His mother (Havana is not Tortuga, and young people have parents there) begged for clemency, overcome by tears, unable to understand what was going on. As there was no executioner now, nor anyone to fill in, he was sentenced to the gallows, in the belief that if there was no one capable of lopping off his head, anyone, they reasoned, could throw a rope around his neck; yet they were forced to delay the execution for some hours because no one managed to tie the knot successfully. Twice the youth was dashed to the ground without losing his life, while his mother roused herself from her bewildered state and began to figure out what to do, first informing the governor that the hangman's knot had not done its work, upon which the governor pardoned the young man, setting it down in writing that if the All-Powerful and Eternal God had permitted the youth twice to escape death, the governor was not one to oppose the divine pardon. Still, the truth was that he, as a Spaniard, did not know how much one is soothed by shedding blood, nor how well this conquers all remorse and reestablishes one's lost peace of mind; he being full of remorse and having no peace because he had killed the messenger and was about to kill an innocent person, but with such bad luck that by the time his letter reached the scaffold the hangman's knot had now been made and the youth was already dead. However, this young man was not the one lamented so pitiably by the mother but another, she having managed to bribe several officials and substitute one of her slaves for her son, a fact never realized by the governor in his remorse because there were too many sons in that house to be able to tell one from another, though, as is well known, if a mother undertakes to do so she can recognize any son she may have.

Will I be able to continue this story without the heart of Smeeks, Le Trépaneur, Exquemeling? Could his eyes and ears endure the shock of the pirate's life without going blind or deaf? I think instead that I should divest myself of all three— eyes, ears, and heart—and in order to describe how life is among the pirates, I should stick with the only weapon given me by le Nègre Miel when he died, when I promised to keep his memory throughout the eternity of mankind; because eyes and ears will be overwhelmed by blood and violence, and heart will not get us anywhere, going around in circles, incapable of following the order of time because for it time does not exist, events intertwine, come together, or are incompatible because all things remain subject to the law of violence, hatred, revenge, disorderliness, blood, and death. . . . I will be able to count on my memory alone in proceeding with my story. From this moment on, Le Trépaneur almost daily would be stained with the blood of those limbs half torn away by cannon shot and that he would have to remove completely—I, Le Trépaneur, sawing off so many limbs that I would be able to put together a large army with those that had been removed . . . an army as cruel and invincible as the one the pirates formed at that time, because the remaining limbs would take on names which would be used later on in the fighting by whoever possessed them:

> Exterminator
> Braconneur
> Passe-pour-tout
> En Rade
> Stonebreaker
> Wingy
> Razor
> Screamer
> Slow Fuse
> Naked Sword
> Feu-de-joie
> et cetera, et cetera

Unless, perhaps, I have not already used more than memory in relating what I have set down.

seven

*T*he following morning, recovered from and with the help of the feasting and from and with the help of the drinking, L'Olonnais ordered the first squadron to inspect the neighboring areas. He did not wish to make use of the Indians on land, and he left them as our rear guard at the lake and in the gulf. Fifty men went out to find someone, anyone at all, in order to discover where all the people of Maracaibo were, but their persistence was futile. Even though they did find a small group and tortured them all, and even though he had one of them hacked to pieces in front of the others, threatening them with the same fate if they did not reveal where their riches were and where the other citizens had gone to, the most he was able to get was directions to another place, and he ordered his men to go there quickly—only to verify that it had already been abandoned *(they having the plains and as a nearby shelter the fortified city),* upon which he ordered the attack on Gibraltar, a town not far distant.

Many of the two thousand people of Maracaibo had taken refuge in Gibraltar, but just as many others, the men above all, fled the latter town every day, terrified that because of the fearful interrogation methods used by L'Olonnais, someone might betray them; so that, just like animals, they distrusted their fathers, their brothers, their children, digging a new hole for themselves every day, suffering hunger and thirst; while we freebooters were enjoying the benefit of their munificent homes and larders. But for L'Olonnais, enjoying merely what they had left behind (of which there was much, a great amount of loot) was not sufficient. He wanted everything; and more than anything else, he wanted *them,* and he wanted to fight. So that two weeks after having landed, we turned toward Gibraltar, loading part of the loot on board together with the few prisoners we had been able to take, and leaving a prudent force in Maracaibo to cover our return. We disembarked a few leagues from the town, near La Ribera. One of the Bravos showed us the way. All worked up, well fed, our knapsacks filled with good provisions and very little alcohol running through our veins, and possessed by a strange mood of childish joy, we seemed like something more than pirates. To take possession of the city without having to struggle for it, to be enjoying the loot without bloodshed, had quickened our blood. Up until the moment of leaving Maracaibo we had not lost a single one of our own men, and we had neither sick nor wounded; though on the road some began to show signs of having contracted a strange fever, but they pretended not to have anything wrong and we pretended not to notice how weak they were. For several days we had been lords while staying in Maracaibo without having fought for it; we had eaten at their tables, the very tables of the previous lords, without having bloodied our hands to do so! So we scarcely gave a thought to the terrible road that would take us to Gibraltar, on the southern part of the lake, where the land became more swampy. The closer we got to Gibraltar, the more nervous the Bravo guide became, as if something odd had happened, or were about to happen, although L'Olonnais interpreted his nervousness as due to the fact that he was plotting something against us, that he was going to plunge us into an affair that would be our ruin; but it was impossible for us to talk to him and discover if he was betraying us because he spoke nothing but his mother tongue. But only by L'Olonnais was the Indian's agitation noticed. The rest of us paid no attention to him, although had it not occurred to us that he was guiding us in error, deceived as we were by a false path the Spaniards had built to entrap us, we would not have awakened in time from so pleasant a sensation, and perhaps we would have lost the battle.

Because suddenly the road we were walking on became so soft to our step that we sank into it, and in our confusion we did not know what to do with our feet, where to put them; but the Indian, without the least hesitation tearing branches from the palms and other trees and casting them beneath his feet, urged us with signs to do the same; and although we saved ourselves from drowning in the fetid mud, for a short while we thought nothing was going to keep us from burying ourselves in these watery lands, because the false path the Spaniards had laid out to snare us ended at the water; yet the clever Bravo guide, without losing a step, turned half around and by shouting persuaded us to hurry, afraid that night would overtake us in the midst of that swamp, which was what the Spaniards wanted. That was when we saw the alligator, that fearful animal, rise out of nowhere. The color of the mud itself, sluggish as mud as well, it surged up from the deepest part of the swamp, moving as if it were flying where it was impossible to travel without clumsiness or feeling itself as heavy as stone—its swiftness doubly astonishing since these animals swallow stones to give their bodies more weight and enable them to hunt their prey in the way they do. The enormous animal moved its huge body without difficulty on its short legs, and, opening its gigantic jaws, seized one of our men and carried him off, plunging deep into the water with him and resting its heavy body on the unfortunate man until he drowned, then returning the body to dry land and depositing it on the sand, ready to come after another of us and kill him by drowning him and then to leave him in the sun to rot, because these animals only eat flesh that is decomposing; but the brave Indian, with only his knife, launched himself fiercely after the animal, killed it, and before our eyes opened its belly for us to see the stones the terrifying alligator carried within its body in order to sink the victims of its appetite.

We retraced our steps and the Indian rediscovered the right path. But at that point the Spaniards were waiting for us with cannons, muskets, and piles of good gunpowder. That was when the event took place that I already have mentioned: They fired so often and in such great disorder (even causing wounds among themselves because of the confusion into which they fell) that soon we took care of them and considered them beaten. In three hours five hundred of them were killed, and ourselves worn out; but not so much so that L'Olonnais would not carry through what he proposed to do when he first saw the Bravo guide had erred: He had him tied to a tree trunk, laid his breast open with a sword, and pulled out his heart, all the while shouting that this animal had almost carried us to defeat, that he was not going to pardon the guide's carelessness, that the treatment he was giving him was exactly what he deserved—and in the light of the bonfire that had been lit to cure the many wounded, I saw the Bravo's eyes looking on with an indescribable expression, with living eyes still, as L'Olonnais ate his brave heart; and so brave was he that he spit in L'Olonnais's face before falling forever, perhaps, into the arms of death. We slept right there, having neither the strength nor valor to leave the field of battle, more afraid of the alligators than of the dead, and as soon as dawn broke we gathered up the bodies. Fourteen of our men we buried there, the majority having been consumed by their fevers rather than by gunpowder gone astray. The bodies of the Spaniards together with that of the Bravo guide were loaded onto two boats and set adrift a couple of leagues into the lake.

Organized into several columns, we entered Gibraltar. Still they defended themselves. First we attacked the monastery situated at the base of the walls, thinking to protect ourselves from the bullets with the bodies of the monks and nuns; and undoubtedly, out of the respect they hold for such persons, the Spaniards would not have fired at us were it not for the shouts of the former: *Death to these heretics! Shoot, so the Lord will gather us unto Him! Kill them! since for Christians death does not exist, but eternal life! Shoot, shoot! Do not be cowardly. Death to the heretics!* They killed them all.

Within the city, the superiority of the Spaniards was still notable. We fought furiously, but as they were protected within their buildings and made all the stronger by their familiar knowledge of the place, they gave us no quarter.

L'Olonnais ordered the retreat.

They scarcely saw we were outside the town when they came rushing out in order to follow us, which is what our Admiral hoped for. There we were able to trounce them, and those who were not killed or did not fall into our hands fled in the din of the battle.

We entered Gibraltar now like furious wolves. We raped the women, we pillaged the church, we destroyed the images, we leveled it all, we took three hundred prisoners, men, women, children, and slaves, and put a price on each one, ransom money for all of them. The majority died of hunger because there was little food. For ourselves we set aside all the cassava roots, as well as the poultry and the pigs, and in order to feed the others we had some donkeys killed; but they preferred to die rather than eat such filthy meat, especially when the worms got into it and it seemed more like swarms of flies than food.

With the prisoners L'Olonnais went off into a fury of cruelty, submitting them to awful tortures so they would confess where they had hidden the great riches of Gibraltar and

Maracaibo, and to verify whether there might perhaps be another army to attack us. He cut off the tongues of those who would not speak, he branded their bodies and cut off their limbs, he burned them or did terrible things to their bodies that left no mark but made their inner organs burst. After having ruled Gibraltar for four weeks, we demanded extortion money not to burn the place down. We asked for ten thousand pieces of eight not to set fire to the town, for lack of which we would burn it and reduce it to ashes. We gave them two days to bring in this sum, and the conquered citizens being unable to scrape it together so quickly, we set the town alight in several places. The Spaniards begged us to put out the fire, and that we did, aided by the residents who came together, but since we had spread tar and oil over the stones of the buildings we had set fire to, no matter how hard we worked we were unable to avoid the destruction of part of it, especially the convent church, which was reduced to dust, down to the foundations. After receiving the money mentioned above, we carried silver, furniture, money, jewels, and goods aboard, together with a great number of slaves that had neither paid off their ransom nor yet died.

eight

The Bravos, their bodies painted in vivid colors, were waiting for us in front of the spot where, under the Spaniards, the governing palace had been located, an esplanade of goodly size, bare of vegetation, in the center of which, on a wooden platform the way they do, the body of the Indian whose heart L'Olonnais had torn out was awaiting us. Women on their knees surrounded him, weeping and screaming, striking their heads against the ground. The men were calling out and shouting, walking back and forth.

In astonishment, we saw this scene from our flotilla, and also the men we had left behind, moored only a few yards out from the wharf, loaded with the booty stolen from the city.

A piragua approached L'Olonnais's ship. In it there came an interpreter from the Bravos who in good French said he had orders from his chief to bring L'Olonnais before him in order to give an explanation of what had occurred (sensible words to which L'Olonnais would not give ear) and ventured to affirm himself deceived by the peaceful L'Olonnais they had known, a quiet man who had seemed like an inoffensive animal; but who, now, as in the midst of a fight, before their very eyes becomes inflamed and turns into a demon, into a fury, a hurricane, and without listening to the messenger, orders a small boat to let our men know they are to bring their ship over to us, and that for no reason will he go to meet the Bravos' chief, for they were nothing but savages while he was a Frenchman and had no reason to explain himself to anyone, much less to the Bravos, who were not in the least brave and courageous since they had been vanquished by those ignorant Spaniards.

The interpreter returned with this reply, and the Indians prepared to attack us.

Fortune was on our side that day; the Spaniards had received reinforcements and followed our progress, we on the water, they on land, having planned a strategy with the aid of Rafael Marques (whom we no longer even remembered), thinking to attack us when we were inside the walls of Maracaibo once more, at the spot which was the weakest point of our position in the city—the very place where the Bravos had been stationed! What must have been the anger of the latter, not only upon hearing L'Olonnais's rude reply but then seeing the hated Spaniards enter; upon which they fell into furious combat. From our ships we launched cannonballs against both parties, causing terrible casualties, greatly increasing the number of dead, and not a few already that they had already wrought amongst each other.

When we set foot on dry land once more, Rafael Marques, wounded in one leg, was waving a white flag and greeted us with a wild tale shouted out of how the Spaniards had made him prisoner and how pleased he was to see us returning victorious, using words that I will set down here, gesturing so wildly that he seemed more like a drunk than a guilty man, more a buffoon than a traitor, for panic had overtaken him and he was unable even to attempt to tell the truth while his exclamations ran on like this: *Brothers! You who obey the Law of the Coast, salve! Long live the pirates and may these corpses die who, because they are Spaniards, deserve to be corpses! To take me as your prisoner, is that not a lack of respect? Because, who am I? I am the vassal of pirate justice! Long live the Society! I raise a toast to you!* Upon which one of our men put a bullet into him so he would never again open that cowardly, deceitful, vile, traitorous mouth whose eloquence did not serve to hide his mean spirit. From the top of the mixed pile of bodies Spanish and Indian, Queen Metecona of Blue Island no longer needed his cloak to reign on earth.

L'Olonnais was not satisfied. He demanded a ransom for the city as well as for the prisoners we were dragging around with us, or at least what was left of them. We had been two months in the Bay of Maracaibo, if what now presented so different an appearance could still be called Maracaibo, when we finally received the ransom for the city. We left then, bound for Tortuga. Our booty was much more considerable than anything we could have imagined.

To get through between the two capes that would let us out into the open sea, we sent to Maracaibo for help, where it is said their fear was reborn and only stilled when they discovered we were merely in need of someone knowledgeable to guide us. There were no more Indians any longer who might do this. We had finished them all off. Along with their women. The children in their huts wept, and when they saw us passing by, if we came close to any of their islands, they threw rocks and sticks at us; for good reason were they named "Bravos," and if they had had any weapons, they would have fought valiantly against us; the poisoned arrows they learned to shoot very young, and shoot well, would have caused many casualties amongst us, were it not that, on the very spot where so many Indians had died, we had made a great bonfire of their weapons.

nine

Two months. Eight weeks. Sixty days. How many hours? When we stopped at the island of Aruba for the Vice Admiral to arrange the tallying of the booty and L'Olonnais to prepare for the safe return to Tortuga, I tried to reconstruct myself with regard to the attack on Maracaibo. It had begun with the taking of the fort, so quickly, I must confess, that the piragua carrying me to dry land had not touched it yet before we were already the winners and the Spaniards the losers. That was where I exercised my profession as surgeon for the first time. I took out some bullets lodged in a thigh, in an arm, in three shoulders, treated knife and sword wounds . . . The city itself we entered without a struggle. After a few days there, I removed a finger and entered that fact in my notes, the ones I would have to turn over to the Vice Admiral when the expedition was finished so he could arrange the distribution of the loot. Now in Aruba, before handing over the summary of arms, fingers, eyes, and limbs lost, I went over the count: the first leg was blown off by a cannonball and I only had to tie off the arteries; the second one I had to cut off because it came to me still attached to its pirate, shattered and blackened by a powder explosion. . . .

My eyes went over the list with which I was able to re-construct the events of the fighting, but something prevented me from making sense out of them. Time, those sixty days, had held me at bay. I was no longer myself; Le Trépaneur was the master of my actions. In my notes, which I ought to reproduce here, were numbered eighty-four legs, but I did not know how I should keep accounts in my person for the mutilated images in the church, or the Spanish women raped, or the meals I had had in huge mansions, or the tortures witnessed. . . . How long had it been since I had been indentured, a slave, how long since I had slept in the open air, on the landing of the house where I grew up and was expelled from? I was unable to reconstruct myself on our return from the attack against Maracaibo. I was no longer anyone but the fist that had wielded the sword drip-ping blood, the eye taking aim, the finger pressing the trigger, although it was not I who had fired the gun and used the sword, I was the bodies that had been killed, often with good reason, when they objected to the fact that we were tearing their works and possessions away from them, and often for no reason at all other than that of watching them die, hearing their bodies fall, splattering us with their Spanish blood; and I was the bodies I had treated, the ones into which I had plunged my scalpel, my chisel, my knife . . . Is this what I really was? Weren't my true parents le Nègre Miel and Pineau, who had taught me those noble, grand secrets? Finally, I was a Brother, like them, a member of the secret Society of the Brethren of the Coast. So this was the way I had participated in the best dreams of the two good men, all the while my elbows dripping with the blood running from my hands. . . . No, I was not able to reconstruct myself. But in my body I felt such satisfaction that it almost blotted out the pleasure of the adventure, that of being a pirate. Had I lost my way? But as I asked myself this, I realized that what I had lost was my body, that I had been only a slave, an *engagé,* and when I was no longer that, I was merely the slave who had lost his body. . . .

I was unable to understand anything. I could not understand why, among the pirates, rape was preferred over the whores, especially when it came to the Spanish women, for whom the humiliation provoked them to struggle so violently and suffer the degradation of their downfall so painfully. Those Spanish virgins, above all—how they fought to preserve their honor! Because when we were through with them, they thought they had no chance of making a decent marriage, and, faced with the idea of finding themselves unhappily married to a man from a lower class, an aged man, a widower, or someone with a repulsive defect, sometimes they preferred never to marry and instead to resign themselves to keeping their saints' images in clean clothing. In Gibraltar there had been a mother, still rather good looking, who with her young daughter remained defenseless in their house when the town fell. The mother feared the well-known excesses of pirates and freebooters and immediately ordered her servant to bring some prostitutes and had her cooks prepare some food, and then she wrote a note saying,

Our strong men have been defeated. This house surrenders, as they did. Since you have conquered, it is all yours, and all the riches it contains. I have even had women brought here for the pleasures which it is said you are so eager for. I am an honorable woman and my daughter is still almost a little girl. We will be the only things that, appealing to your feelings (which I am sure you have), we request be respected.
Cordially yours,

La Marquesa de la Poza Rica

Since this was one of the two most splendid mansions in the town, it was taken over immediately by the pirates; and we were received in it as if we were gentlemen, welcomed with drinks, food, comforts, and women, with a huge party that had been readied with all the trimmings. When L'Olonnais, seated at the table, asked to whom they owed such a fine welcome, a servant brought him the note written by the good woman. He had not even done reading it when he gave orders to look for them, saying, *Do not take anything from this house, freebooters, because what is fit for the cattle should not be of any interest to us if there are two pearls here with which to reward us!* The servants and the whores tried to convince us to the contrary, but they only managed, with their persistence and their attempts to thwart the search, to earn their deaths. The house was turned upside down. They tortured a boy horribly so he would tell them where their mistresses were, but it was a futile torment, because he managed to die without saying a word, after being castrated and much of his body flayed, with huge chunks of his skin torn from him.

Someone had the notion of setting fire to the house, but the Admiral discarded the idea, saying, *These stupid women would prefer to die in the flames rather than surrender in our arms!* It was only a coincidence that revealed to us the spot where they were hidden. On the second floor, when three men at once leaped up to pull down the fabric that covered the ceiling, behind which we thought they might be hiding, their boots came down sharply on the floor and stove in a slat by the corner. Looking down, one of them saw the gleam of an eye struck by a beam of sunlight that a fallen mirror had sent there to betray them. On taking up the floor, we discovered the two beauties, and with much scoffing, joking, and fondling that they tried to shake off, we took them down to the Admiral. We all stared at them—they really were a pair of pearls!— the mother in her haughtiness, the daughter in her gleaming freshness. The mother spoke in Spanish to L'Olonnais, and thinking that he did not understand Spanish, since he paid no attention to her, began to address him in French, with poignant words and an impeccable accent:

"Admiral, in accepting you as conqueror, I offered you everything in the house, and I personally prepared for your reception, about which I believe you will find nothing to complain. Since I know that you are a gentleman, I have only one request, that you respect us—me, because I am an honorable mother who has never known any man but my husband, and my daughter, my greatest treasure, who as you see is still almost a little girl. I beg you once more, although this house is no longer in a proper state"—she was looking around at the destruction brought about by our search——"for the reception you have deserved."

"Marquesa, we are not cattle and we do not enjoy eating mud and grass, but we are accustomed to pearls. As you put it in your note, you are two of the finest gems this house possesses. We will touch nothing in it, not the money that we have found hidden away, not the silver, not the provisions. The only things we will take will be the two pearls."

"Captain! I beg you, use me, then, but let them leave my daughter alone. I implore you!"

"Hold on, madame. Entreaties merely make L'Olonnais angry, and begging makes him furious. You are not to give me orders, you are Spanish and you have been defeated . . ."

And the dialogue went on in unhurried fashion, until the women, realizing themselves lost because the men were now raising their skirts with the points of their swords and ripping the fabric, tried to flee; and there in the midst of all the commotion, in front of everyone, including the girl's mother, L'Olonnais gave it to the daughter while someone else did the mother, and I don't know how many followed after them, one relieving the next, and when this gang was done they had other pirates brought in to keep on banging them. The abuse was so great that they were left scratched, torn where they weren't bleeding (I saw it myself), like raw meat, with open sores in their private parts and surrounding flesh. When we all left, mother and daughter set fire to the house, I do not know where they got the strength, nor do I know how they could even get on their feet (even less do I understand how one of the two could possibly have wailed, screaming like a madwoman, again and again, I do not know which one it was, *Fuck me, pirate! Fuck me, pirate! Fuck me, pirate!*); and there they died, the same day we finished raping them, the same day the freebooters turned them from prudes into whores, from whores into spoiled meat.

The assault on Maracaibo lasted for two months. In four days on Aruba we finished totaling up the booty and weighed anchor in order to distribute it en route, as the original Contract provided, since before putting in at Tortuga we were to touch at a port called Île-à-Vache on Hispaniola, in order to sell the merchandise.

L'Olonnais, with the Vice Admiral, the surgeon, and seventy of the bravest, set sail a day earlier than the rest of the fleet, aboard a sloop, the fastest ship, carrying none of the booty but very well armed, to scout the way to Hispaniola and, if needed, to clear it of enemies, as we feared an ambush.

Just a few hours after having left the rest of our men the lookout called out "Ship ahoy!" to announce a warship that possibly may have come in search of us. We quickly came up with it and got it to follow us, circling Aruba at a distance to get it away from the booty our men were guarding, and leading it back to the island again but at the opposite end from our point of departure. It was nearly nighttime when we touched land once more, and even though we had left the Spaniards behind, we weren't so far away from them that our other men were out of danger yet if the Spanish ship should start hunting for them once they lost track of us. We anchored the ship and disembarked, together with the sloop's artillery, in piraguas we had gotten from the Bravos. We went inland somewhat, hiding our cannons and our persons in the thickness of the underbrush, in a darkness that was not total because the moon still tinted the sky blue and the branches an opaque gray, even though it was not full and consequently did not give off an intense light.

The dwellers of the forest did not seem to be frightened by our presence. We heard them rustling, together with the leaves and the small branches, and sometimes they brushed against the coarse bark of the trees, slid over the sand, or slipped around among the smooth rocks, though such words seem to exaggerate the miniscule movements we perceived, as if the animals were moving in their sleep, amid their dreams, as if our arrival had not even awakened them. Like many of the other freebooters, I was afraid of alligators, for which reason I had picked up a dog in Maracaibo for company, but on this occasion I received orders to leave him aboard ship, shut up in the empty hold, where we knew he already felt at home and also that he would not start barking amongst the rats, and even if he did bark there it did not matter much; this was a wise order on the part of the officer because the murmurings of the underbrush would have made the dog nervous and he would have made so much noise that, even though I might pick him up to calm him, my anxiety would have left me ashiver and my heart doing nothing but turning flip-flops.

The Spanish frigate approached quietly along the coast, thinking us asleep, because our sloop gave no sign that we were awake. The moment it came sufficiently close, we assailed the enemy ship with all our guns, taking it by surprise; to do this in the darkness made up for their superiority of strength, for in their consternation they did not know whether to fire at the sloop, at the piraguas which they must have gotten sight of by this time, or at the sky, because it never entered their heads that the pirates would attack them from the protection of the trees and underbrush.

We won, as might be assumed, and at dawn, accompanied by lurid bursts of the Antilles sky, L'Olonnais accepted the enemy's surrender, without their discovering until much too late the conditions of their defeat: in less than an hour, or a period of time that seemed very much like it, L'Olonnais had put them all to the sword: the commanding general of the foot soldiers, Captain Don Pedro de Avellaneda; the Admiral of the Fleet and Field Marshal, Don Gonzalo Suárez Ossiz; the Sergeant Major and captain of one of the companies, the battalion captain, the captain of artillery, their adjutants, the standard-bearers, the chaplains, the royal lieutenants, the quartermaster, the keeper of supplies . . .

Although it was not very convenient for the return of the expedition, we were forced to take their frigate for our own, as the sloop had been damaged; and we sent a piragua that skirted around the island and warned our other men of the change, waiting for its return in order not to go ahead reduced not only in speed but also in strength, while we tossed overboard everything of any weight carried by the frigate, leaving only the meager ship's stores, which turned out to be our booty, and making room for our cannons.

When the piragua returned, it bore a youth who had been caught red-handed; when one of the Brothers had embraced him he felt some hard object under the young man's belt and ordered him to show what he had because this was his matelot and thus obliged to obey him; and when he refused, he was beaten until he was forced to reveal it to the Brother: a heavy necklace of gold and rubies that he had found somewhere in Maracaibo and had not handed over to the Society for the just and equal division of the loot. L'Olonnais had the thief brought before him. In front of all of us he cut off the little rogue's nose and ears. I cauterized the wounds with le Nègre Miel's herbs. We put him on the frigate, and the day of our departure we abandoned him on an islet with a wineskin of water and a musket with powder and balls for his only company. The best thing the thief could have done with them would have been to blow his brains out before going through a prolonged agony and death in the middle of the immense ocean when the tides would have covered the little bit of earth that sustained him! No one felt sorry for the sailor because he truly deserved the punishment.

In eight days, with no other interruption, our frigate in the lead, then the fleet of pirates slightly behind, we reached Île-à-Vache, where some French buccaneers live who sell dried meat to the freebooters as well as to the merchants who come there for the purpose of doing business with the freebooters.

We unloaded what we had taken, even the bells of the church in Maracaibo and the images and paintings, and the five hundred head of cattle. We divided the prizes amongst us, according to the agreement in the Contract. After having tallied everything up, we found 270,000 pieces of eight in cash. Once this was parceled out, everyone received pieces of silk, linen, and other things to the value of more than 100 pieces of eight. The wounded, many of them mutilated, received their portion first: for the loss of a right arm, six hundred pesos or six slaves, for a left arm five hundred pesos or five slaves, for a right leg five hundred pesos or five slaves, for a left leg four hundred pesos or four slaves, for an eye one hundred pesos or one slave, for a finger the same as for an eye . . . Then all the silver was weighed, figuring ten pieces of eight to the pound. The jewels were appraised at varying amounts because none of us had the slightest knowledge in the matter.

We passed on to the distribution of what fell to those who had died in battle or in some other way. Their portions were given to their friends to keep, so they could hand them over to their heirs eventually.

Once the distribution was concluded, we set sail for Tortuga, arriving there one month after having put in at Île-à-Vache, to the great joy of the others because many of them no longer had any money. When we landed on Tortuga, the merchants were already waiting for us.

And the prostitutes. The tavern keepers. The gamblers. And every other species of fauna capable of fleecing us in exchange for the grand fiesta.

The night that had begun during my earlier stay on Jamaica had not ended, it simply moved to Tortuga.

Nothing to complain of in that: our night is fiesta time. Our men arrived on the heels of two ships loaded with wine and liquor, the booty from other pirate raids, peddled in Jamaica and transported to Tortuga. On those first days the alcohol was worth as much as sunlight or cattle feed on the islands; ten days later it was ten times as expensive, and in ten days more its price multiplied a hundred times, raising its value from that of pasturage to gold, although the moment it passed down our throats it seemed just the opposite: those first days, something like a golden sun resided in our bodies, radiating light, like a candlewick, an artificial, twinkling light by which to cruise through the fiesta; and as the days passed it turned into a hard, gray stone deep inside, almost black, ensconced in our viscera, our blood, our muscles, darkening us more and more, as if it were getting us used to the surrounding night.

During the course of those days, we were very much accustomed to go in for table games and to bet on them, and to pay high prices to rent the cards and gambling tables.

The musicians who had gone with us on our raids fell silent here, while others rendered jolly songs, and you heard them wherever you were. I think they never stopped playing the whole night through, because I never stopped hearing them. Here and there, too, was heard the strange music of the African slaves.

The women of The House journeyed from Port Royal to be with us. They had improvised a little theatrical display for a welcome. As the curtains opened, they appeared in fixed tableaus, done to perfection in all their details. Among the freebooters I heard it said that some recognized the tableaus as reproductions of famous paintings and considered them quite exact, above all *The Death of Dido,* by Vouet, being the one that was most admired; it was said that such skill had gone into producing this one because Madame (as a child, now that I think back to her) had been the painter Vouet's lover. I can say with certainty that one of the tableaus was exactly like one we had stolen, and it caused great laughter in us that what had made the Spanish breasts so fervent while it had hung on the walls of the church in Maracaibo now had its Virgin represented by our prostitute, its Joseph by the whores' footman, the Child in the manger by a very serious hen who appeared to be setting on eggs, its Sainte-Anne by a girl we had screwed one night . . . After that, in beautiful pavilions improvised among the rocks and trees of Tortuga, after the manner of the Arabs, they gave themselves to us to satisfy our carnal appetites.

Here and there some were eating in sumptuous style, consuming dishes that seemed touched by fairies and sorcerers who had put their hearts into their flesh, which our whores never managed to do.

ten

⁂

*T*he banker takes up the cards, three packs together, and shuffles them. He has Braconneur, to his left, cut the deck, and then calls out, *Ten pieces of eight.* Le Tunisien, to his right, answers with *one real,* and gradually, one by one, the *ten reales* Van Wijn has asked for is reached. He turns up a card, his own, a three of clubs, and without pausing, turns over the next one, alongside his card and to the left: the "points," an ace of diamonds. Immediately he turns another, and everyone begins to shout: it is not a pair with either the banker's card or the other, that of the points. He turns another. The points start shrieking: *Ace of diamonds! Ace of diamonds!* They squeal and wave their arms around. The place seems like a pen full of restless animals. Like pigs when pirates come in to get supplies for their voyages, whether or not their owners want them to, and if not at first, they will after being beaten. Pens so full of pigs, so crowded with pigs they cannot even move. They squeal again! A double blow! *Three of clubs!* Van Wijn wins. The banker.

He shuffles again. Braconneur cuts. *Thirty pieces of eight* is the call. Le Tunisien responds with *three reales,* and nine others follow. He turns a card: seven of clubs. Agitation in the pen: a bad-luck card. For the points, the banker turns over a nine of diamonds. The first card after those two is an ace of diamonds. The banker loses.

He leaves the game, but before going he pays his fee to Benazet, a Frenchman, who owns the cards and rents them out and gets richer every moment with his gaming business, at the expense of the freebooters. No one regulates the games on Tortuga, and, there being no taxes, he passes on a fixed amount to the governor and piles up the rest. He does not drink. He has no wife, and women are of no importance to him, at least not if he has to pay to have them or maintain them. He does not care about eating. He does not pay the musicians who play in the gaming house. When he is the banker he always wins. The only luxury in his place is an inscription mounted on one wall adorned with flowers and vases bearing the legend, *Gambling provides us with the various pleasures of surprise.* An army of slaves cultivates the fields around his gaming house with plantings of tobacco; they dry it and then, down on their knees, they roll it, and he sells it at the price of gold because it is said to be very good tobacco. The fields belong to no one on Tortuga, he simply uses them without even paying for the use.

Benazet calls me aside, to threaten me over something I do not understand. I have not been playing today, nor drinking. In the morning I showed two youths how to make bandages. But I have been watching this good fellow Benazet because everyone who deals with him loses. He makes threats against me, again and again. I do not understand what he is talking about. His voice gets louder and louder. The "points," the banker, all the domino players look up, removing their attention from their games to watch what is happening. He blusters even more, unaware that everyone is watching. I do not comprehend the course of his harangue because my understanding is focused on what it is they are staring at, on observing the faces of the Brothers and the burgeoning anger of Benazet, a wrath such as I never imagined in his wily person. He threatens me again, letting fall a word that is like a blow to the face: *Pineau.* My vision clouds over. Blood pounds in my ears. My legs want to move but they refuse to obey even themselves.

I am not the only one who has responded so forcefully to the word. Behind the wave of blood that has clouded my hearing, I do not know how I manage to hear the chairs falling to the floor, the dominoes clattering, the blows . . . No shouting, no words, no whispers, none of the restrained milling about in the pigpen as there was during the game. The gates are wide open and they are all out of there like a shot.

Against Benazet and his supporters, the ones who help him out, but who now would rather run off than continue to help him out. The Brothers against Benazet.

When they are done, I see Benazet tossed on the earthen floor of the gaming house. Made into mincemeat. The Brothers embrace me, one by one. In absolute silence.

I break into tears while they continue to embrace me. Someone brings me a glass of sweet wine to ease my pain, and tells me, *We took care of him. He won't get you the way he did him. No need to be afraid of them, they are cattle.*

Right there, before me, Pineau's murderer, dead.

With the wine in my blood, I went over to the already abused body, and I kicked it and kicked it, gone all notion of time, until there was nothing left under my feet but a foul mass, something like a pile of vomit, almost a mess of pottage, and the tatters of his clothing floating like chunks of bread in the soup: I was Le Trépaneur, and that thing had been the murderer of the two men who taught me how to be so.

While I was quenching my anger and nourishing my grief with my boots, most of the Brothers had started their games once more, but a small group was searching for the place where Benazet kept his money. When they discovered it, they turned it over to Antoine Du Puis, the Vice Admiral of the Maracaibo expedition, for him to add to the booty and distribute around to us, thus prolonging the fiesta into which had entered this strange ray of light from the revenge we took with the death of Benazet, the Frenchman who had never been anything but that filthy mess to which he was now reduced.

This was my revenge, though I did not understand yet why Pineau and le Nègre Miel had died at the hands of the crafty, unscrupulous Benazet.

This was my revenge, but although it gave vent to my heart, it never managed to rise above the level of my ankles, or at least the ankles of my understanding. In spite of that, even now sometimes, when I recall this story in order to bring le Nègre Miel back to life, I seem to feel once more the greasy mass that shithead Benazet was turned into by the blows of the Brothers and my own incontinent feet. But oddly enough, that slimy mass, while being revived by the memory below my ankles, does not make my equilibrium any the more slippery or inse-cure; but instead my step is firmer because of it, more certain; and the odor that rises from it causes the blood I can no longer make run through my veins seem to move back toward those elastic days, each of them a night after I signed my name to the Law of the Coast.

eleven

*T*he next thing we sold to keep the dissipation alive was a ship loaded with cacao. The fortunate buyer was the governor himself, offering the twentieth part of what the whole lot was worth.

The moment had arrived for those of us of the Coast to open our wallets to each other. We saw this happening not only amongst ourselves, but also in all that was going on around us: the women of The House folding up their pavilions and stealing away to Jamaica, the improvised dining rooms with their succulent banquets disappearing as if they had evaporated into thin air, the merchants robbing us by offering trifles for magnificent articles . . . Before being completely cleaned out, whoever had a single coin left would share it, because that is the way pirates are, generous with each other: open pockets. Or that is the way they used to be before the coming of the Second Fifty.

The First Fifty was the Spanish one: roving attack groups comprised of fifty men each and divided into squads that continually moved around through the forests of Saint-Domingue to surprise and attack the buccaneers in their burrows. Fifty at a time, they managed to root out the uncouth buccaneers from the northern part of the island.

The Second Fifty descended on Tortuga, and it was a disaster just like the first. Luckily, it was not a case of several fifties but only one, yet it was as harmful to the Brethren of the Coast as the earlier one was for the buccaneers.

But I have to give the reader fair warning: If I were to relate to you right now what this Second Fifty was like, and their devastation of Tortuga, its early end, and the discovery it brought me concerning Pineau and le Nègre Miel, this story would come to a halt here and now. But if I keep returning again and again to my tale, that is simply to fulfill the promise I made to le Nègre Miel on his deathbed: to undertake to make his memory live. And I still wish to describe the well-deserved end of the brutal L'Olonnais, not wanting to leave *him* alive; nor do I wish to leave myself in those turbulent seas, I want to get myself back to Europe, where today—if I am still any place at all—I am telling these stories.

Going back to where I was, then: When there was no longer a single one of us with a coin left in his pocket to keep the party going, we dogged L'Olonnais to organize another brilliant assault; and while he was working on that, some went out in canoes to raid the turtle fishers, others went to sea to try their luck on their own (with such bad fortune, it is said, that the moment came when they got hungry enough to raid the humble residents of the coasts just to get hold of their cassava flour and dried fish; and it was so bad sometimes that even these impoverished folk would manage to push them out of their homes without yielding them a thing), others went to Hispaniola to procure sufficient supplies, and still others, those with L'Olonnais, careened their ships to get them ready for the next expedition.

When the Caribs prepare for war, they throw *ají,* a kind of red pepper (somewhat like pimiento) on burning coals, provoking a sharp cough and an irritation in the mucous membranes, which they believe produces the state of mind needed to attack with sufficient fury. We pirates did not resort to *ají* or pimiento, nor did we go in for the wild dances that finally succeeded in inflaming the Caribs for their battles. We managed to achieve the state of mind needed for our assaults by feeling our empty pockets, our dry throats, the weariness of the fiesta that had been going on for weeks, and the satiety produced in us by the prostitutes, those women who had nothing for us written in their gaze and who took part in and gave support to the explosive outbursts provoked by our moods (if we had any) in order to achieve something that seemed like a calmness of mind based on a foundation of alcohol, gambling, plenty of food, and music; and they were in luck indeed if any of us paid them to actually perform, without some kind of stratagem, the labors characteristic of their office; since when it came to women, as I have already mentioned, the pirates preferred those who needed to be forced, women who resisted them, as they found pleasure in the humiliation and even more pleasure in extreme violence. One pirate (whose name I will preserve in silence so his soul, surely in difficulty even now, does not come after me for revenge) enjoyed killing the woman he was possessing, saying that her flagging flesh squeezed him in such a way that there was no greater delight than to have a woman die while being used; and there were many who tried it out to confirm this, some of them agreeing, others not, and still others who said they found it a pleasure only if the woman was killed by someone else.

Who, then, knowing the nature of our pleasures, would be surprised at the character of our assaults and our warfare? And who, with a knowledge of these, could imagine us to require any roasting of *ají* on burning coals to become galvanized? Yet whoever was aware of these things would still never understand that these men went through a definite alteration of feelings and sensations, depending on whether it was before an attack, during the fighting, or afterward, whether with loot in their pockets, or just after having squandered it, or . . . Although for the moment, what with the shock of this forceful reminder of Pineau and le Nègre Miel having been imposed on me by Benazet's threats and his death, and the need to be preparing my surgeon's supplies for the upcoming expedition because our departure seemed imminent, I kept myself to one side of these emotions, something apart from the body formed by the pirates as one whole being, warm and always ready and willing; yet was I well able to understand that we freebooters *were hopeless; what could we do on shore with our pockets empty if we knew not how to slow the descent of someone sliding down a hill, someone without relief or remedy? When we would be awakened in the middle of the night, after too much alcohol, by its racing uncontrollably through our veins, being too much for them, we would wonder: How could people live on dry land, shut in behind four walls, and how could they resist the hopelessness of the red-tinged evenings of the New World, and how, without the breadth of the ocean, the water without borders, without corners, without banks or ports . . . ? Because on the high seas, or in pulling down what others had raised up to shut themselves in behind, our freebooter hearts found the only places where we were able to drain off that abundance of intoxicated blood running through our veins!*

    Before we were able to put a stop to the feverish turmoil of the taking of a city, before we were able to suspend that delirium and see it as a thing apart from ourselves, even before we learned to tell ourselves the battle was over and that we had become rich because of it, by then we no longer had any money of our own, no longer a new shirt or a length of silk or linen or even a bit of common cloth! Nor did we realize that the end of that story had already caught up with us when we felt the necessity surging up of undertaking yet another assault somewhere. . . . The afternoons, then, raised the red banner of the attack, every afternoon, and each dawn as well, that huge banner waving before our eyes; and although others might not understand what this impassioned red thing was, all enveloped in the colors of the Caribbean Sea, we knew the red was the signal for a fight, that we pirates would have to keep on fighting, destroying, that our time was not yet done with, not quite . . . that we had to go on with a musket in each hand and a knife clenched between our teeth, although we were already being phased out, feeling everything as occurring too late, escaped from time, the only certain thing for us being the dark, drowsy wrath of the alcohol, since even though completely submerged in it, the pirate never for-

gets that, before all things, he is one of the Brethren of the Coast, as Mansfield discovered during the capture of Santiago, an inland city. After he had taken it, when they had already brought in and piled up all its riches, the freebooters launched into celebrating their triumph in Santiago itself, sharing the glory with the defeated inhabitants. They got everyone drunk, young and old, even the children, by making them gulp it down right from the barrels that had been made there to sell. With the conquered city in a state of intoxication, they forced the rich to dance for the amusement of the poor, and made them also parade their daddy's little darlings around in loose, open dress, an invitation to be stopped and screwed by whoever (drunk and shouting) wished to. They ripped the buttons off the pants of the governor (for whom they had already received ransom money) who yet went around everywhere, fully drunk, shouting orders, trying to impose order with his pants at half-mast and slurring his words, since he could hardly speak for all the alcohol they had forced him to drink.

Still in a fervid state, the pirates undertook their retreat laden with copious loot, making their way toward the beach where they had left their ships; but a party of sober citizens under command of the still-intoxicated governor tried to stop them and would have been able to do so were it not that Mansfield and his Brothers, though enveloped in the cloud of rum that obfuscated their movements, were still living through the moment of the struggle when, making such good use of their wit and their forces, they had figured out how to make Santiago theirs in the first place. They had another exchange with the Spaniards and kidnapped the governor once more, and both sides began shooting until all their guns fell silent: both sides had run out of gunpowder. Then they launched into all sorts of invectives, the pirates demanding a new ran-

som for the governor; but there came a moment when they no longer heard any reply: the Spaniards, weary of the verbal war, were not answering; they had withdrawn.

Mansfield and his men, not knowing whether they were in the middle of the first assault, the celebration, or the later fighting, with their nerves on the alert like those of every good pirate, went on their way to the beach, boarded their ships, and just as they were about to set sail, received a miserable amount for a second ransom of the governor. Never had a governor brought so little or been so poorly dressed, what with his pants so stubbornly determined to remain on the ground! Thus it was that although Mansfield in his jubilation had celebrated his victory too soon, yet they were unable to get the better of him, not even when inebriated, because he was still able to fight fiercely when in that state; nor was there the slightest trace of intoxication in his judgment, nothing of the lush, the souse, the tosspot, boozer, juicehead. Not like there was in Rackham, an Englishman who lost his ship to an English attack when they encountered him and all his crew totally drunk—even though two women fought to save him: Anne Bonny, capricious and rich, and Mary Read, clever but impoverished before becoming a pirate. Although we Brethren of the Coast ought not to be mentioning this, for it happened long after we had already been dissolved, when Exquemeling had been thirty years dead, when even Port Royal, the port of opulent pleasure, had already been swept away by the waves—yet why should we not bring it up here, since our sluggish pirate's consciousness is also an instantaneous awareness, which, like our reactions, positions itself outside of time? . . .

With our spirits inflamed, then, our lack of gold having turned each of us into passionate, blazing flesh, and in that

sense, dried-out and thirsty flesh, we pirates hastened to prepare for the next assault:

꧁꧂

During the night it was when they found themselves separated
from the other ships. Lack of skill? Winds that forewarned of
those to come later on? Better for them if Lord Hurricane had
come down upon them before they met us! Better to be de-
voured by the waves than find themselves alone off the island
of Guadeloupe, in a tight bay whose entrance to the sea was
surrounded by high reefs, carried there against their will by some
current they had hitherto thought provident!

   We had gone out aboard a sloop in search of canoes
because L'Olonnais had decided on the site of our next assault,
and with its being approachable only through shallow waters,
the attack would have to be made in canoes, the which were to
be taken by those of our party from the turtle fishers, even
though these folk were never armed and had no other belong-
ings than their poor canoes. This was not a pleasant task and I
do not have the slightest idea why I joined them. The remain-
der of the freebooters awaited us on Tortuga.

   "Ship ahoy!"

   The Second Mate gave orders for our sloop to draw in
close to the Spanish galley, waving the red flag that demanded
their surrender. In the blink of an eye we would be ready, on
the edge, eager to board their bulky ship with so unusual a crew
and passengers: the Archbishop arguing hotly with the Captain

without listening to reason; the officers giving orders right and left, most of them contradictory; the Second Mate panicking and gone mute. The Archbishop, not knowing what we were like, was demanding that they fight the pirates instead of merely fleeing inland and abandoning everything but their skins, as the Captain wanted. I am not certain whether he was cowardly or wise because although they were well armed he knew they would be defeated; for the soldiers who had custody of the Archbishop and his riches, instead of carefully and eagerly preparing for the fierce battle that was upon them, were simply complaining at the top of their voices about being separated from the rest of the fleet, while the galley slaves were deaf to the confused orders they were being given and kept rowing slowly and in disjointed fashion, moving the galley in a bizarre pattern, clumsy and pointless.

As soon as we came close enough to examine their deck, the musicians on board broke out in a dissonant racket, everything out of tune, as loud as they could. At the outbreak of that mangled music, we all began dancing on our own deck, the Captain in his tattered doublet with its gold brocade, his threadbare silk hose, and a hat trimmed with crumpled plumes, the rest of us shaking our rings, bracelets, and pendants, kicking out our legs, waving our arms to this side and that, occasionally shooting into the air. There we were, dancing, when the two prows bumped against each other; thus with musket in hand, knife between teeth, and having opened a breach in our sloop's hull so there would be no way of turning back, we boarded the Spanish galley.

The Archbishop, erect, dressed appropriately as suited His Excellency, interposed his enormous crucifix between his person and us while he prayed in a loud voice and we rushed against the benumbed, cowardly soldiers who cried out for mercy here and there without even putting up a resistance. In a matter of minutes the ship would be ours, ours the gold cross mounted with precious stones, ours the Archbishop's trappings.

But suddenly we heard a terrifying bellow, something like a scream or a howl that surged up out of the cargo hatches, outdoing the volume of our musicians: the galley slaves, despite being still in their chains, fed up with the rowing officer's whip and his brutality, and aware of our boarding from the Spaniards' nervous confusion, took advantage of his bewildered state and seized that officer who had so mistreated them until that moment, and then passed him along from one man to the next, gnawing chunks from his body and devouring them bite by bite, until he was hardly anything but bones, and, in the end, lifeless—which was when that frightful howling came to an end.

The booty was so abundant and the galley so useless for hunting down the turtle fishers that we thought to return to L'Olonnais as soon as possible, yet one of our men prudently urged us to wait because in the strong breezes of the previous night he believed he saw an early warning of other more forceful and hardly tamable winds: a hurricane. And even though we did not believe him in all conviction, such fear did the mere word "hurricane" put into us that we listened to him, though not to the letter, unfortunately. Because he advised us to move with all our booty to dry land, having the island so near, and look for a cave or dig a shelter, leaving the prisoners to sink with the galley but taking with us the two canoes we already had acquired in order to return to Tortuga, and to come back later for the booty. Oh, if we had only obeyed him in every detail!

twelve

What fist was it that had cast all these islands on this sea the way one sows seeds: shaking and opening all the fingers at once? The Caribbean is sown with islands great and small, lavishly populated by islands, unpeopled and primitive, subject to the fact that the owner of the fist that sowed the transparent sea might send a fearful wind to turn it into a Massive Ocean, an indomitable wind which, even though everyone knows, of course, that it may be repulsed by a few here and there, appears to have been tamed by no one: the terrifying Huracán, the god of the Indians who once peopled these islands: Huracán, never to be trusted.

When it comes, the sun turns to water and the transparent waters cloud over, torrid and angry, as if the winds of Huracán were stirring them up from the bottom, as if down there the winds were roiling them, as if Huracán were transforming their element, as if the winds were able to make them rise: and they, infused with a wrath like that of young women who know not their own strength, pant after anything they see and devour it, gulp it down, transformed from their normally limpid, translucent clarity into a gluttonous digestive system, into acids that dissolve anything they consume, into brawny muscles, into oily, slippery, mucus-like, corrosive apparitions. Take care, freebooters! Something more fierce than you are has been set loose! It is coming to seek you out; Huracán has no fear, the waters of the sea have a sudden need for flesh, and Huracán knows not who the pirates are: but even so he is coming after you, you who think you have no other master than God nor any other law than force nor any other will but violence! He is coming after you!

We were left without the galley, without the Archbishop, without the Archbishop's crucifix (the wind took it off as well), without the galley slaves, since in all the turbulence and with every chain welded to the boat they went down with it; and almost without ourselves, because most died. Those of us who went ashore to sleep were safe; we had lashed the canoe to the largest trees, and as soon as the weather calmed down we set out to join the others at Matamaná on the southern coast of Cuba where a great many turtle fishers live and where L'Olonnais would probably be, rounding up canoes. And so he was. It gave us great joy to find ourselves together again with the other Brothers, thinking that here would be the end of our poverty and tribulation.

We set sail for Cape Gracias a Dios, located on the mainland in the same latitude as the Isla de Pinos, but once at sea we were overtaken by a sultry calm: no longer beloved by the Caribbean. Had we been touched by Huracán? Water and wind were now both contrary, and our food supplies running low. By canoe we found an estuary and went in search of food and water, stealing it from the Indians: a store of corn, livestock, and chickens, yet not enough for the enterprise we had planned, thus continuing to cruise along the coast of the Gulf of Honduras seeking more provisions; yet in raid after raid on the impoverished Indians we never got enough together for all of us for long and we would finish off what we had previously collected before we got the next batch. Then we came to Puerto Caballos, a Spanish market center with warehouses where they store all the merchandise that comes down from up-country until the arrival of their ships.

We captured a Spanish ship and, not to arouse suspicion, used it to approach the mainland, taking over the two warehouses and all the buildings in the town, and also taking many of the inhabitants prisoner. L'Olonnais inflicted the most awful tortures on them, so viciously that when I asked permission to heal the body of a poor woman tortured severely, a woman whom he had decided to leave alive, not from compassion but out of cruelty, simply so she would continue to suffer the agony his vindictiveness had brought her, in response I was asked whether I considered myself a surgeon or a veterinarian, since she being Spanish, my intention to treat her was just like a veterinarian would do, because treating her was like treating animals. Yet I could not withhold my compassion, and to avoid a clash with L'Olonnais I gave her some poison during the night so her soul might greet the dawn without that body so sorely abused by his extravagant persecution.

When all the prisoners were dead we went toward San Pedro Sula. Only three leagues had we gone when we found ourselves in an ambush that, although it caused us many mortal casualties and wounded, was yet unable to resist the fury of our response. L'Olonnais had the injured Spaniards who remained on the path finished off after he asked them for what he wanted.

Three more ambuscades we beat off, since there was no other road where we could avoid them, until at the very entrance of the town the Spaniards found themselves forced to raise the white flag as a signal of truce. The conditions for surrender would allow the inhabitants two hours to pick up everything they were able to and flee.

We entered the place and spent two hours standing around while the whole town of San Pedro Sula was hiding itself and the citizens carting off everything they thought they could carry.

When the time was up, L'Olonnais had them followed and whatever they were carrying taken from them, and then he turned San Pedro on its head. But there was no way to find everything they had hidden, so after staying there for some time, celebrating after our fashion, we reduced the place to ashes.

In the midst of our whooping it up, which was much wilder than when we returned to Tortuga from Maracaibo, I discovered a woman lying at the foot of a wall and moaning feebly, her request for water the only sign of her need for help. I turned her face and body toward me, pulling her by her long hair because I did not want to place my hands anywhere that might hurt her. What I had in my hands had once been a head and a body but now was a mass of flesh mutilated along its full length: cut and burned, whipped and beaten. I wanted to give her something to drink but found no lips on which to rest the vessel, and so with my knife blade I let some drops fall on her bloodied tongue. How was she able to utter it, *water, water*? And who had done this to her? Had someone of ours put her to torture to get her to confess something, I asked her. And she told me, *No. But I have something to tell you. Soon a ship loaded with treasure will pass along the coast.* All this she said, I know not how; nor what lips, tongue, or mouth she used, for of those she had none. After which she died.

The same news was received from other bodies found by me or others here and there in San Pedro, bodies that had once been children, men, women, though whoever had taken them to this hideous extreme seemed to enjoy making them all alike, without distinction of rank, sex, or age.

For three months we waited for the arrival of the ship, living together with the wild Indians of Puerto Caballos, hunting turtles with a certain bark craft called *macoa,* and driven to despair. When we finally captured the ship, we did not find what we were waiting for, as it had already been unloaded of whatever it carried of value, the great treasure advertised consisting only of fifty iron bars, a little paper, some containers of wine, and things of that sort, hardly important at all. Those bodies, tortured by some of our men, had lied to us.

After that attack, we gathered for a vote. L'Olonnais proposed that we make our way to Guatemala; the most disap-

pointed of us, new to such exercises, had believed that pieces
of eight could be plucked from the trees like pears, and now
they left the company. Others, headed by Moses Van Wijn,
returned to Tortuga, to continue under the orders of Pierre le
Picard.

A few of us decided to follow L'Olonnais without knowing that we were voting to watch his ship run aground in the
Gulf of Honduras, too big to slip through the ocean tides or up
the river; and shortly afterward, in the islands called Las Perlas,
it foundered on a sandbank, where we took it apart to rebuild
it in the form of a longboat with which we thought our luck
would change.

While we were tearing it down and reassembling it,
concluding that here was labor enough for some time, we cul-
tivated some fields, planting beans, Spanish wheat, bananas. And
thus, during the five or six months we were in Las Perlas we
ceased bearing any resemblance to pirates, so much so that we
even kneaded bread and baked it in portable ovens.

Eventually half of those of us who were left embarked
in the longboat. In a few days we reached the estuary of Nica-
ragua, where, to our misfortune, Indians and Spaniards together attacked us, killing many of our men and forcing us
to flee toward the coast of Cartagena, where L'Olonnais fell
into the hands of the Indians of Darien; and what happened
to him there will here be set in the mouth of Nau himself,
L'Olonnais, the son of a small merchant of Sables d'Olonne,
who let himself be signed up by a colonist from Martinique
passing through Flanders, on a three-year contract for the

West Indies, and whom he left, slavery seeming unbearable
to him, by escaping with some buccaneers by whom he was
beaten and mistreated and picked up by yet others who enlisted
him into the Brethren of the Coast; and he led the glorious
expedition to Maracaibo, only to undertake the unsuccessful
story in which he lost his life, in this fashion:

*We took the boat in toward shore, toward the jungle, to try
hunting, since in this land there is little more to be had than what can
be found in the jungle. We would attempt to discover game; and while
the others were preparing for this, I left them and went on ahead for a
short reconnaissance unarmed, thinking the place deserted. As I pushed
along through the brush, suddenly on both sides of my path I heard a
great shouting, as the savages are in the habit of doing, and they sprang
toward me. I saw then that they had me surrounded, pointing their arrows
at me and shooting. I exclaimed, "God help me!" and scarcely had I
pronounced those words when they had me down on the ground, throwing themselves on me and poking at me with their spears. But they only
wounded me in the leg, and I thought, "Thank God!" expecting that
at any moment my own brave boys would be coming for me. My assailants removed all my clothing. One of them took my shirt, another my
hat, a third my boots, and so on. They began to fight over me, one of
them claiming he had been the first to reach me, and in this way they
pushed me through the jungle down to the ocean where they had their
canoes; and where I counted myself lost, as my men had not arrived.
When those who had attended the canoes caught sight of me pushed
along by the others, they ran to meet us, adorned with feathers as is
their custom, biting their arms and forcing me to realize that they wanted
to eat me. Before me stood a king with a club that is used to kill their*

*prisoners. He made a speech and told how they had made me their slave,
wanting to avenge on me the death of their friends. And when they took
me toward the canoes some of them kept slapping me. They hastened
then to drag their canoes out into the water, fearful that my men might
be alarmed by this time, as was true enough, while others bound me
hand and foot; since they were not all from the same place, each village
was annoyed that they would have to return with nothing, and they
argued with the ones who were keeping me. Some said they had been
just as close to me as the others, and they also being eager to have a part
of me, proposed to kill me immediately.*

*I waited for the blow, but the king who wanted to possess me
said that he wished to take me home alive so that the women might look
me over and have some fun at my expense, after which they would kill
me, they would make their special liquor, and everyone would get together for a feast and they would dine on me conjointly. So they left it,
binding me at the neck with four ropes, and forcing me to get into a
canoe, which was still beached. They tied the ends of the ropes to the
canoe and then dragged it into the water for the return to where their
huts were. Suddenly, I realized that I was understanding the words of
their savage language as if they had spoken them in my own tongue.
And consequently that there would no longer be any deliverance.*

*Coming to land, they pushed the canoes up on the sand, where
I remained as well, lying down now because of the wound in my leg.
They circled around, with threats of devouring me.*

*In the midst of this great affliction, I remembered the glory I
had once enjoyed, and I also saw before my eyes the bad luck that had
been pursuing me since leaving Tortuga the last time. With my eyes damp
from weeping, I began to sing the psalm "My God, My God, Why Hast*

Thou Forsaken Me?" which I had not sung even once since leaving childhood behind. Nearby were their women, in a field of manioc close to the sea. And I was forced to call out to them in their language, "I am your dinner, and now have I come!" and while saying these words I imagined that it was those of their sex who were to blame for the bad situation I found myself in—without knowing why I thought that.

They lit bonfires as soon as nighttime arrived, and arranged me in a hammock, my arms bound just as the hammock was bound to the poles holding it up. They hitched the ropes that went around my neck to the highest part of the tree and lay down all around me, talking and calling out, "You are my little creature, all tied up!"

At dawn everyone ran out from their villages to have a look at me, young and old. The men came with their bows and arrows, commending me to their women, and then led me away with them, some ahead, others behind me. They were singing and dancing the songs they usually do when they are about to devour someone.

In this fashion they brought me to a kind of fortification situated facing their huts; it was formed of long, heavy tree trunks, rather like a wall around a garden, and is useful against their enemies. When I entered the enclosure the women ran at me, slapping me and pulling at my beard, shouting at me in their own tongue, "In you I will take revenge for the blow that killed my friend, murdered by those who were with you!"

They led me afterward to a hut and forced me to lie down in a hammock. The women returned and went on slapping and pulling and tugging at me, telling me they were going to eat me. One woman approached with a piece of glass fixed in a bow-shaped stick, cutting off my eyelashes with that bit of glass. Then they wanted to shave off my mustaches and beard but I did not let them, until they brought some scissors left them by the Portuguese.

They began to prepare the special liquor they were to quaff after eating me. The fire was ready. They did not roast all of me whole but one part at a time, first one limb, then another . . . I was still alive when I saw even the children devouring parts of my body, chewing on chunks of my flesh, until the loss of blood made me lose consciousness, and my last breath left me the moment they drove a stake into my body as a spit for roasting torso and head together. I did not feel the fire. I do not know how the ceremony ended in which the Indians of Darien celebrated the feast provided by my body.

thirteen

During our unsuccessful expedition there was a moment when, during the night, the memories with which le Nègre Miel peopled the darkness of his blindness began to rise up out of the nothingness.

I saw a lioness springing upon an antelope and devouring it. I saw the ostriches running over the savannah, the dense plantings breaking through the gray earth, the odd way they dressed their men and women, the way they painted their bodies and faces with many colors. I saw animals I do not know how to put names to, huge and strange and not always fearful. I did not know right away that these were le Nègre Miel's memories, but as they kept recurring and became purified through the years I gradually realized that they were not mine, that inscribed within me, carefully assembled, as in a paradise, were the recollections of le Nègre Miel.

Even now, in that blindness which the passage of the centuries has presented me with, and which I am so grateful for, le Nègre Miel goes on making his way around that valley where the earth reaches its perfection, showing it to me as more perfect every day, as if it gets better and better the oftener it finds itself being repeated. The men, the women have now disappeared from those pictures. Only plants and animals reside there, plus that beautiful beast we call the earth, shining in the most miraculous cloud formations, its rivers, its mountains, the rustling of a breeze whispering nobly, continually . . .

We returned to Las Perlas and ran into good luck, a freebooter's ship bound for Jamaica having touched there. From Port Royal, after visiting the women of The House to attend to their indispositions and problems, I returned to Tortuga, now terribly depressed. The island that awaited me was different. The Second Fifty had fallen upon it, Tortuga being changed from stem to stern, and not for the better. Bertrand d'Ogeron, he who was hated for a thousand and one reasons, had gotten what he wanted. In my absence, a ship with fifty females had arrived and the governor had them up for sale. Whoever purchased one could not take more than one, and that one had to be taken to wife. By the time I arrived he had sold eighteen females, three of whom had already left their husbands, with the latter now embroiled in a wrangle with d'Ogeron over the return of their purchase price. But the buying and selling was not what was disturbing the atmosphere on Tortuga. Each of the fifty women had taken possession of a *boucan,* those huts held in common which the Brothers of the Coast would normally stay in whenever they returned from an expedition, or else they would make use of some slave to build another; and now they had nowhere to lay their bodies down for sleeping except on the rocks and sands of Tortuga. Further, the females had decided they must be sold together with the *boucan* they were living in, so they could fix it up and arrange it to their liking, and the slaves were forbidden by the governor to cut trees or branches to make others or they would suffer the whip (with the excuse of managing the forests, as if there were anything to manage): all of which, without raising the price they might have brought without the *boucan* (there was no price on the cabañas, for they belonged to all), favored the interests of the governor who had had them brought from France, declaring them orphans mercifully released from an orphanage, so that the uncouth Tortuga men would change their adventuring life and settle down.

One had only to take a single look at those females the governor was advertising as orphans to doubt that such was their case: rather, they were trash taken out of La Salpêtrière, though not from the Mazarin section or the Lassay building, but from the heart of the institution, from La Force, the prison; and if one knew nothing of that and had only observed their behavior or listened to their language, which was so dissolute that it was surprising to find him persisting in his false claims, it would have been instantly clear that they were not simply destitute females but prostitutes lifted straight out of the mud first and then from the chains and subterranean jail cells of La Salpêtrière. Nor were they like the beautiful women of The House and the other brothels of Jamaica that our eyes had become accustomed to. Poorly nourished, and that is saying it too kindly: half dead from hunger, actually, and well along in years, they were more like dogs in a drought than women. Anyone would bet that none of them would have been sold. . . . Yet, as the days went by, twenty-seven more of them managed to get themselves bought. . . . But before getting to those twenty-seven that were sold after my return, I must come back to repeating that although everything seemed to have changed on Tortuga, and that much really had changed, still one tavern apparently had survived just as it was before my last departure, and I took shelter in it with the expectation of sleeping in a cave that many of the Brothers had taken as a dormitory, not far from Cayonne.

I did not have a copper in my pocket but the Brothers took me under their wing and invited me to eat and drink, the pirates being, as I have said, ever generous with their own. Besides, they wanted me to tell them about L'Olonnais's end and about the bad luck that dogged our recent ventures, just as I wanted them to tell me about Tortuga. Very little had I managed to relate, though by this time I had mentioned my desire to hear the news about what I had already seen on the island, when Jambe-de-bois, an old pirate and one of the men on the Council of the Society, moved quickly in my direction, holding out his bowl with both hands. He thrust it against my body, almost shoving it into me, looking me steadily in the eye without removing that insistent wooden bowl from my belly, and said *Excuse me!* out loud, while in a very low voice that he concealed behind a blow of his wooden leg against the floor, in order to obscure it from the others, he whispered, *Here, take it!* I held on to the bowl and moved away hastily, and suddenly I heard a shout: *We are cattle but you are pigs!* with several voices at once screaming out, *Pigs!* and then very quickly came three shots in a row, hurled from three firearms. I did not raise my eyes to see where they had come from because my eyes were following the body of Jambe-de-bois sinking to the floor, and as I watched him go down, something guided my eye to the bowl he had shoved at me to take. In the bottom was a folded piece of paper. I picked it out immediately and stowed it discreetly beneath my clothing, against the skin, and continued staring at the scene without moving.

With the words *Le Trépaneur, look to him,* someone in the midst of the commotion pushed me toward the injured man. Others were trying to get at the group that had attacked him.

The sound of the shouted *Pigs!* still rang in my ears. I walked over to Jambe-de-bois and bent down to check him over. He was dead. A bullet had gone through his heart. I said nothing but left the tavern. I started walking inland, where there were no buildings, treading the paths that Pineau had loved so and that le Nègre Miel had covered so many times looking for herbs and roots for his cures. Yes, I too, like Pineau, loved the island. Mixed emotions were moving me, stirring my heart. Pineau and le Nègre Miel, my two fathers, had died here, and this was my land.

I do not know how much time passed as I walked around, caught up in the emotion brought on by that word *pigs.* Suddenly, I recalled the piece of paper Jambe-de-bois had served up to me in that bowl. I sat down on a rock, listening intently to see if anyone had been following me. Nothing was heard but the buzzing of the flies and bees and the passing of the wind through the leaves.

I drew the piece of paper from where I had put it and unfolded it. There were actually two pieces, one of them a long, narrow strip, the other a full-sized sheet covered with tight handwriting. First I looked at the long strip, in the fading light of the oncoming night. There were many rough sketches, but all quite clear: a white man screwing a black man, a black screwing a white, with them grasping each other by the hand; the white man screwing a black woman, and the black man likewise; the woman holding the white man by one hand and the black man by the other; the black man, the black woman, the white man, and a mulatto child; the black woman with a dagger in her breast, buried there by the black man; the mulatto child and the white man in a ship inscribed with this legend: *Lord of La Pailleterie with the son of Louise-Césette Dumas*. In the next sketch there was a white man screwing a black man and a black man screwing a white; and the last sketch was a small map of Tortuga.

I did not understand a thing. In larger letters, toward the lower end and below all the drawings, could be read this legend:

PRO PHE CY: IF WO MEN ARE NOT PRO HIB IT ED THERE WILL
COME A DAY WHEN BRO THER WILL MUR DER BRO THER
AND THE PO WER OF THE FREE BOO TER WILL END.

And in smaller handwriting in the corner, this appendix: *Those who are loyal to King or Cardinal are not people, they are cattle.*

Very carefully I coiled it up and put it inside the other, folded sheet, just as it had come. Why had Jambe-de-bois given this to me? It was getting too dark to read any more. I went back and found the Brothers in the cave. We performed the rites of the Brethren, all of us eating from the same loaf of cassava bread, and singing songs in which we swore eternal loyalty to each other. And drinking.

In the same spot we kept vigil over Jambe-de-bois's dead body. No one spoke of avenging him, but they did speak of not buying any of the women brought by the governor. I did not mention the papers, nor did I cease to think about the prophecy.

Yet, as I have already mentioned, twenty-seven more women were bought, the majority by men who had still not been initiated into the Society, matelots whom we would expel for that reason before they got to be freebooters. But there were also two of the older Brothers, something I was unable to explain.

It was rumored that they, with connections to the governor, had been Jambe-de-bois's murderers. Even if they were, the count was not exact. I had heard three gunshots. Who was missing?

Had I known for sure, I would have killed the three of them by kicking them to death, pounding their cattle flesh as they deserved.

fourteen

When I finished reading the document written in the tight, neat hand of Pineau, I was moved, and also contrite. Why had I not been aware before? How was it I had entered the Brotherhood in a cloud of alcohol to take an active part in that marvelous dream without knowing that I was part of this utopia of great hearts? How was it that I had benefited from many of those aspirations without being shaken by the thrill of it, simply turned into a brute animal being fed choice tidbits without understanding or enjoying any of them, without knowing that I formed a part of what the girl on the ship (my beloved *she*) had told me about as we voyaged from gloomy Europe to sublime Tortuga *(In the lands we are going to, I have heard it said that there is no "yours" and "mine" but that everything is "ours." And that no one asks, "Who goes there?" and no doors are secured with locks and chains, because everyone is everyone's brother. I have heard this said. And the only rule is that of loyalty to the Brothers. To be one of them you cannot be weak, a coward, a woman. I will go to a nearby island and see if*

I can fit in with that better life)? But it all seems to be read now in some other way because the ambitiousness of a few of them (piglets who dare to call themselves hogs) did its best to turn their faces away from it, because on Tortuga "yours" and "mine" and "Who goes there?" are now alive and well, because even though Benazet the owner of the gaming enterprise is dead, there were now three others just like him that I was unable to kill because I did not know who they were, and still others powerful and wealthy who were well protected and who would not let anyone take "theirs" away from them. Even worse, with gambling they dulled men's desire for adventure, drawing them back to land, clipping their wings with the false battlefields represented in the card decks and chips, turning their wild energy into straw to feed the fires of their riches. . . . Now they let themselves sign on with the governor in exchange for a few coins to pay for their card games that take the place of their adventures, or to allow them to bring home a few trifles for their women.

The dream of the Brethren had come to an end, and I saw no way we could make it live again.

The last one to sign the document was Jambe-de-bois, and now he was dead. With the knife I carried at my belt, I punctured the tip of my thumb and signed the document with my blood, trying to keep my name readable, "Le Trépaneur," shaping the letters with the knifepoint.

I kept it beneath my belt, flush against the skin, and carried it there for years, until I lost it during an assault from which I have never been able to explain how I got out alive.

Thirty more years did I spend in those islands after having signed the Law of the Coast, not among those magnificent men for whom there was no other law than that of God, but among pimps and muggers of the lowest sort who accepted the policy of paying taxes and tribute to d'Ogeron, to his nephew and whoever followed them, puppet governors who represented a king from beyond the sea. If I resisted living together with them, it was because I knew that they were the unworthy heirs of a magnificent dream that allowed men to take what belonged to no one by any legitimate law, and because the wave that formed out of that dream, though drenched in violence or alcohol, one or the other or both, gave me something that no other kind of life was able to. I must confess this to be so, now as I write these pages with the eyes, the ears, and the heart of J. Smeeks, Le Trépaneur, to keep alive the memory of le Nègre Miel, I who have had a run with the good fortune of preserving the remembrance of a place where the earth reaches its perfection.